More praise for *The Detective Is Dead* and Bill James

"An excellent and alarmingly realistic novel, violent but never indulgent, the plot driven by spare, witty dialogue. The characters are all too plausible."
—*Sunday Independent*

"A compelling read." —*A Shot in the Dark*

"Bill James is a frontrunner among those who have turned the police procedural on its head. . . . [Harpur and Iles] have procedures and a wicked style all of their own."
—John Coleman, [London] *Sunday Times*

"Bill James's Harpur and Iles books are deliciously unsavoury: a brilliant combination of almost Jacobean savagery and sexual betrayal with a tart comedy of contemporary manners. A stylized world that is several moves from reality, and about as real as you can get." —John Harvey, "The Crime Writer's Crime Writer," *Guardian*

"[The books in the series] all add up to a stunning history of how crime has changed the fabric and character of British society." —*Publishers Weekly*

The Detective is Dead

The Detective is Dead

Bill James

W. W. NORTON & COMPANY

New York • London

First published 1995 by Macmillan London Limited
Copyright © 1995 by Bill James
First American edition 2001
First published as a Norton paperback 2002

For information about permission to reproduce selections from this book,
write to Permissions, W. W. Norton & Company, Inc.,
500 Fifth Avenue, New York, NY 10110.

Manufacturing by the Courier Companies, Inc.

Library of Congress Cataloging-in-Publication Data

James, Bill, 1929–
    The detective is dead / Bill James.—1st American ed.
        p. cm.
    ISBN 0-393-05019-X
    1. Harpur, Colin (Fictitious character)—Fiction. 2. Iles, Desmond
(Fictitious character)—Fiction. 3. Police—England—Fiction. 4. Drug
traffic—Fiction. 5. England—Fiction. I. Title.

PR6070.U23 D47 2001
823'.914—dc21   00-048975

ISBN 0-393-32246-7 pbk.

W. W. Norton & Company, Inc.
500 fifth Avenue, New York, N.Y. 10110
www.wwnorton.com

W. W. Norton & Company Ltd.
Castle House, 75/76 Wells Street, London W1T 3QT

1 2 3 4 5 6 7 8 9 0

The Detective is Dead

Chapter 1

When someone as grand and profitable as Oliphant Kenward Knapp was suddenly taken out of the business scene,
you had to expect a bloody big rush to grab his domain,
bloody big meaning not just bloody big, but big and
very bloody. Harpur was looking at what had probably
been a couple of really inspired enthusiasts in the take-
over rush. Both were on their backs. Both, admittedly,
showed only minor blood loss, narrowly confined to the
heart area. Both were eyes wide, mouth wide, and for
ever gone from the stampede.

Colin Harpur knew them. Of course he did. It was his
job to know them. Easy. It had also been his job to make
sure they did not get killed, or, if not exactly that, to
make sure when they did get killed the people who killed
them were caught. This should ensure a good, all-round
reduction of the active villain list. For a start, these two
would no longer be on it, obviously. Also, you could cross
off however many were put away for doing them. But
to put away those who did them required unterrorized
witnesses and an unterrorized, unbought, undemented
jury, plus a judge ungutted by famous overturned convictions and ready to treat police evidence as different from
shit. Less easy.

The Chief and Assistant Chief had come down to view
the bodies, proving the deaths were emblems. Top ranks
dealt in overtones. These corpses proclaimed that on this
police force's patch, and on most other patches, gangs ran

their rivalries, wars and settlements regardless of the law. Everyone knew this, even Mark Lane, the Chief. He honourably yearned to stop it and pretended to believe he could. That was for morale, his own and his team's.

Iles crouched in the rubble squinting at the two corpses with a flashlight. 'Possibly as small as .22 bullets. Magnum rimfire? Pathfinder? At least two wounds in each. At the most, .32. Panty-hose revolvers, from the States, sir. Britain's stiff with guns of all shapes since border barriers came down. The Met say five thousand in London alone.' The ACC glanced up at Harpur. 'Oh, you'll get nowhere with this one, Colin.'

'How, how can you say that, Desmond?' the Chief cried, his voice bouncing sharp and damning around the bare room, like the wrath of God.

'Nobody saw anything. Nobody says anything. Everybody's scared,' Iles replied.

'But can we tolerate that on our ground?' Lane demanded. 'It is people's duty to tell us what they know, and our duty to act on what they tell us, and then to protect them.'

The ACC gave a wholesome, lavishly grateful smile, radiant even in the drab light. 'Colin, whenever we feel dirtied or crushed by the foulness of our work, we turn to the Chief for affirmation of true values.'

Lane had been off work with a full breakdown, and two expertly killed pushers in a derelict, boarded-up, Valencia Esplanade house must seem a poor way to start a comeback. As for Harpur, he was used to sessions among the stinks and dust of these once select homes, ogling casualties.

The Scene of Crime people and photographer arrived with their gear, and Mark Lane waved a fond hand towards them. 'Are you telling me – us – this is all a useless charade, Desmond? Our efforts? Never! Those responsible for these deaths must be swiftly caught and brought to justice. I'll have no gang rule here. This force has attracted enough hostile notice from Home Office and Inspectorate of Constabulary. We *will* show we have control. At once.'

Of course, behind Lane's protests would be the suspicion, always that fierce, ravaging suspicion, that Iles, and possibly even Harpur, wanted no true investigation because he, or they, knew more than they showed; maybe had a gainful corner in the dark commerce that produced these deaths. Lane saw himself as tragically alone, isolated and kept ignorant in his eminence. He mistrusted everyone, and especially Iles. Those reasonable, black uncertainties had pushed him at last into outright depression three months ago. On the day Lane went off ill Iles had said: 'The sod felt so solitary his mind split in two to give himself company, Col. But it wasn't viable when total, so what chance for halves? Collapse.'

Now, Iles said, 'I know these two deads, don't I, Harpur? Lovable laddies both of them, in their turdish, grab-all ways. Alby Horton, Josh McCallion? Horton's the bigger grin, sir. He was proud of his teeth.'

'Know them?' Lane replied. 'How know them? First names?'

'We've had them in, Col?'

'Now and then.'

The Chief said: 'As to clearing up this appalling situation, I am quite sure Colin and his team will be—'

Iles stood and thoroughly brushed down his suit. 'This is how it goes, sir: Kenward Knapp's shot in a gang tussle during your unquestionably deserved sick-leave, so there's a gorgeous realm suddenly on offer – say seventy per cent of the drugs trade in our manor, and half the top class receiving. Maybe some pimping. This is mighty, non-taxable money. Think of Kenward's house, The Pines. Big Merc. The momentary vacuum after his death brings its own battles and its own silences. Who bosses these two, Col?' Iles asked.

'Whoever pays,' Harpur said. 'Anyway, all sorts are

3

trying it alone now, since Kenward's firm came up for bids. It's part of the nationwide small business drive.'

The Chief said, 'But—'

'And then, sir, suppose Colin here, by some of his fine, filthy magic, gets an informer for us, finds a secret way around the brick wall of fear and greed. What's next? Some fucking old ponce wig will insist from the Bench that we not only name the tipster but produce him to give evidence and face cross-examination.'

The Chief kicked away three half house bricks so he could stand more solidly on even ground before taking on Iles. 'Well, Desmond, I do feel that under this country's justifiably admired legal system a judge has the right to—'

Iles said: 'So either the informer gets blown away by one of the accused's aunties before reaching court, or is executed on contract afterwards. Hundred grand price ticket. Grasses know the way it goes at trials these enlightened, everything-open days, so they no longer produce, do they, Col?'

'Not as once,' Harpur said.

'And if we drop a case to protect our informant, the gangs know what that means, so he gets snuffed out anyway.'

Lane wanted to leave. He turned towards the one doorway where the boarding had been removed. Then he came back. 'Perhaps acting without such aid is healthier, cleaner, more professional,' he said. Now, his voice trembled with resolution. The lay-off from work and from Iles might have built him up. 'I've always despised the whole damn informant carry-on. As you know. To deal with the tainted is to become tainted ourselves.'

Iles pulled out a leather-bound notebook and very slim gold pencil. 'Do you mind if I make a note of that, sir?' he replied. He intoned as he pretended to write laboriously: *To deal with the tainted is to become tainted ourselves.*

Lane began to leave again, then once more returned,

4

his voice still determined: 'Besides which, there is an established, official code for dealing with grasses, yet I am bound to deduce from what you say, Desmond, that this is continually flouted here. It is central to the proper handling of an informant that he or she is deemed to belong, not to any one officer, but to the police service as a whole. There is a laid-down structure of Handler, Controller, Registrar. You apparently speak of Harpur as having his own, private sources, and speak of it compliantly.'

'You know Harpur, sir,' Iles replied.

Chapter 2

'To put it briefly, then, Detective Chief Superintendent Harpur, these two deaths, Albert Horton, Joshua McCallion, took on something of a symbolic quality, did they not?'

'I don't know what you mean.'

'I think you do, but let me explain. I want his Honour and the jury to understand exactly what I am saying. Were not these two murders regarded by you and your superiors as signs that an escalating gang war had broken out on what you would call your ground?'

'I can't answer for my superiors. To me, these were two men who had been shot dead. That was all.'

'And because their deaths were seen as so significant, you were under exceptional pressure to make arrests, were you not?'

'Whenever someone is murdered we try urgently to find those responsible and bring them to trial.'

'Is it not the case that a notorious drug dealer, Oliphant Kenward Knapp, had recently been killed, and that you and other senior officers feared you were witnessing a ruthless battle between those determined to take over from him?'

'A man called Oliphant Kenward Knapp was killed. We had no conclusive evidence that he was a drugs dealer or he would have been prosecuted.'

'You wished by these arrests to demonstrate that the police still had control, did you not, and were not mere spectators to a war?'

6

'I knew of, know of, no war. My duty was to find who killed Albert Horton and Joshua McCallion.'

'Yours had been a troubled police force shortly before these deaths, had it not?'

'Troubled?'

'Was it not subject to outside inquiries – by the Home Office and Inspectorate of Constabulary?'

'There had been inquiries. No irregularities were discovered.'

'If you please. But I suggest that such reflections on the competence of the force would bring a level of stress to you and your colleagues, and a wish to restore and guard the force's reputation at all costs. At all costs.'

'No irregularities were discovered. No loss of reputation had occurred.'

'I suggest you were under orders to achieve convictions for the murders of Albert Horton and Joshua McCallion quickly, to allay any further outside unease.'

'I would wish to achieve convictions for all murders as quickly as possible, to prevent repetitions.'

'I suggest that the evidence you bring against all three accused, but particularly against my client, is insubstantial, speculative, and much of it mysteriously derived.'

'It is firm evidence or charges would not have been made.'

'Do you understand what I mean when I say "mysteriously derived", Chief Superintendent?'

'No.'

'I thought perhaps not. Or perhaps so. Let me take you to a point in your evidence-in-chief. I have it here: "In company with Detective Chief Inspector Francis Garland I called at the home of Leonard Claud Beyonton and told him we wished to ask some questions about the deaths of Albert Horton and Joshua McCallion." Mr Harpur, why did you believe Mr Beyonton could help you with your inquiries into the two deaths?'

'I had certain information.'

'Where did that information come from?'

'I'm not in a position to say.'

The judge stirred. 'What does that mean? That you don't know, or that you will not say?'

'I am unable to say.'

'Will not say?' the judge asked.

'I am unable to say, my lord.'

'If I may help your lordship,' the lawyer said. 'Chief Superintendent, you are unable and unwilling to say because you wish to protect your source, is that not the case?'

'The source was private.'

'The source remains private, is that not so, Chief Superintendent?'

'Yes.'

'Thank you. You were acting on a tip from an informant, a so-called grass, or tout or snitch or snout, were you not?'

'It was a private source.'

'So we gather. May I take you now to another point in your evidence? "I told Leonard Claud Beyonton that I had reason to believe he had recently begun to associate on a partnership basis with Harry Foster and Gerald Michael Reid," the other two accused. What reason had you to believe that, Mr Harpur?'

'I had certain information.'

'Where did that information come from?'

'The source is private.'

'Is this the same private source as in the previous piece of your evidence?'

'The source is private.'

'Am I right in saying that this source, or these sources, will not appear in court to give their evidence personally?'

'Yes.'

The judge stirred. 'What does that mean? That he or she or they will or will not appear?'

'Will not, my lord,' Harpur replied.

The judge leaned forward. 'Mr Couzel, are you and the other defence counsel content with this?'

'We are not, my lord. Absolutely not. I was about to make a submission to your lordship on this matter. And in this I speak for my learned friends also.'

In the pause, Harpur glanced back from the witness box to the body of the court. Iles had come in to hear the afternoon's evidence. He met Harpur's eye, and with one hand held his nose while the other pulled an imaginary lavatory chain.

The judge said: 'Ladies and gentlemen of the jury, I'm going to ask Counsel to see me privately in my chambers for a short while to discuss certain aspects of the case.'

'All rise,' the usher bellowed.

When Harpur looked again, Iles had gone.

Chapter 3

The party was at Ralph Ember's club, the Monty, in Shield Terrace. Ember would have stopped it if he could, but what hope once it got going? The three of them arrived noisy and cavorting, with a little crowd of relatives, friends and women only five minutes after he had opened up for the evening, and before he knew a thing. They were yelling for champagne, so he guessed something special, and thought it must be about their murder case, but had no idea what, except they were free. And then they started crowing what a prime gem the judge was, so dimpled and sweet-breathed, and what a beautiful banging Harpur took in the witness box – and saying even Des Iles slunk out, knowing it was ashes. Ember began to get the outline.

'They had to pull it, Ralphy,' Claud Beyonton said, his little mouse-face bright as icing. 'We're fireproof. Here's my pricey lawyer, Charles Couzel. Charlie did a scathing job. This is the club owner, Charles, Ralph Ember, almost BA, sometimes known as Panicking Ralph, but it's a disgusting lie.'

'Pull it?' Ember replied.

Couzel said: 'Many judges now see that in an open society it is intolerable for the police to use evidence unsupported by witnesses. In this case, the police refused to expose their informant and dropped the prosecution. That's noble of them, I suppose. But any anonymous informant has to be suspect, must be tested.'

'I love judges,' Beyonton remarked. 'We'd like to send him something. An illuminated address.'

At this stage, Ember did not mind too much that they had come here to celebrate. It was a valid occasion. Not Guilty meant Not Guilty however it happened, and no matter how guilty they were. Anyway, Beyonton and Gerald Reid were paid-up members of the club, so Ember could not have kept them and their guests out. At the start, there were only about twenty, nearly half lawyers, and they spent very nicely and behaved very nicely. Of course, they were loud and would probably get louder, but that was understandable. Three of them had just dodged a life sentence. Three of them had a very nice future. As Beyonton said, fireproof, or near it. Who'd have the gall to take them in for anything again? Not even Harpur and Iles. Who could get the evidence if grass evidence was ruled out for ever? These three had the keys of the kingdom. Ember, gazing at them across the bar, saw potentially very favourable associates for himself. In fact, he should probably feel grateful they had picked the Monty for their rave.

But the word went round fast – word about the collapsed trial, word about the Monty celebration. During the night, the numbers jumped, continued jumping. So many in the City suddenly realized how helpful it might be now to beef up a friendship with these three heroes, Beyonton, Harry Foster and Reid. Spending stayed grand, grew grander, and Ralph had to ring for extra bar help. His champagne stocks might not last. There were toasts, more toasts, a table-top speech by Gerry Reid, who had this renowned mouth. Obviously, he compared the three of them to the Birmingham Six and the Guildford Four, framed police victims, and did a brave, injured performance which climaxed in honest weeping. Two lots of network television arrived for interviews and shots of the party, plus newspaper people, big-wheel newspaper people in today's jolliest modes, not local.

About now, Ember began to worry. Christ, he dreaded publicity, this sort of publicity. He hated some of the talk he heard – swagger talk, give-away talk, threat talk, fuck-Harpur-and-Iles talk. Christ, he did not like so many tainted members here at the same time, nor so much acclaimed pussy. This was not the Carlton Club but Ralphy did strive to keep the Monty in touch with respectability, more or less. In living memory, it had been a meeting place for genuine professional and business folk, a refined spot. Admittedly, the membership had grown rough-house since then, but the point was they did not usually all turn up at once, so the mahogany and brass fittings from that previous life had a chance to proclaim class. Not tonight. Too many. Above the alcohol and smoke he smelled a smell he knew and worked at forgetting – cells. Ember felt glad his wife and daughters were not here.

Gerry Reid, on the table, his cheeks bright with tears, was saying most sincerely into the cameras: 'Friends, one thing I know you would all want to ask us. It's, do we feel bitter and do we want revenge? And the answer is no, no, no.' The words were clarioned. 'We have anger, yes; resentment, but not bitterness. And as for revenge, would we go down to the level of that piece of evil who fed the police slander about us, and would we sink to the level of police who believed it? Never, never, never. Somewhere tonight there's a filthy grass who is sick with shame and fright because we are free and because he knows what we must be thinking, and what all of you must be thinking too. Let him alone with his dread and his poison. They will suffocate him. Our vengeance is not needed.' This brought a kind of applause and some shouting.

Harry Foster, at the bar, leaned forward and said to Ember: 'You think we're bloody lucky, yes, Ralph?' Harry was with his girl, Deloraine.

'I think *I'm* bloody lucky to get your party,' Ember replied.

'Where else would we go?'

'Thanks, Harry.'

Deloraine said: 'Who do *you* think, Ralph?'

'What?'

'Put the lying word to the police.'

'It's an industry,' Ember replied.

'Harry thinks someone's really inside a business concern,' the girl said. 'Someone with rare knowledge. There was detail, authenticity.' Harry punched her arm almost lightly and she said: 'Mind, that doesn't mean the stuff was correct. But you know, genuine insight.'

'I understand,' Ember replied.

'Knew the whole Kenward Knapp operation and just how these two, Horton and Josh McCallion, tried to grab a big share,' she said. 'Horton's so old to try something like that, finish like that. I mean, called Albert. Albert! What century is that, for Chrissake?'

'Clumsy, useless bastards,' Harry said. 'They were in the way, that's all.'

'That Kenward operation needs some handling,' Ember replied.

'It's not impossible,' Harry said. 'Experience. Those two, a couple of beginners, even though Alby's old. Greedy know-nothings. Only nuisances. They were bound to go.'

'How I saw it,' Ember replied.

Deloraine said: 'Well, experience. You've got some of that, I heard – all directions, Ralphy.'

'Thanks.'

She bent across the bar and kissed his cheek, fingering the long scar on his jawline. 'You look like Charlton Heston, you know, Ralphy, when he was younger. Anyone ever told you that?'

'You must be joking,' Ember replied.

'Of course they've told him,' Harry said. 'Get your boobs out of his mouth, will you?' He wrenched her back by the arm he had punched. 'Harpur shows here some nights, yes, Ralph? And even Iles.'

'They won't come tonight.'

'No, not tonight. Not with muck on their face. But before. When they were here before, you see them talking to anyone, Ralphy? I mean, really talking, deep talking? Or going off with, more likely – a quiet chat somewhere else?'

'Oh, these are just terror calls they make here, Harry,' Ember said. 'Supposed to be about the licence, but they collect free drinks and look at who's in, throw their weight about. They don't talk.'

Gerry Reid, with a magnum of champagne in his hand, fell from the table and brought down another where people were drinking. A couple of women got soaked and jumped up screaming curses. Gerry stayed on the floor. Somehow the bottle had not broken and he giggled and took another drink. Beyonton went over to him in case the men at the table turned heavy. Beyonton was small but barbarity made up for it.

'Well, they talked somewhere with somebody,' Harry said. 'But the great thing is this, Ralphy – the better the stuff police get from a grass, the more the judge wants the grass in front of him. If it's just flimsy rubbish, he couldn't care less. But good information, he has to get all mean and fussy, flap his integrity about. Police can't win. Beautiful.'

'I suppose it's all still there, waiting,' Ember replied.

'What?' Harry asked.

'Kenward's operation.'

'Naturally it is,' Harry replied.

'You ever seen that great house Kenward had, The Pines, Ralphy?' Deloraine asked. 'Stables. A gallery. A gallery! And the clothes that cow of his Constance wears – wore. Never the same twice. Some name for a cow like that. This was an operation, the Kenward operation.'

'Just sensitive managing needed, that's all, Ralphy,' Harry said.

'Ralph knows about management,' Deloraine said. 'Well, look at this lovely club.'

14

Beyonton pulled Gerry to his feet and took the magnum from him. They came and joined Harry and Deloraine at the bar.

Ember said with a grand laugh: 'Claud, my view is Harry thinks the leak could have come from inside the Monty itself. I'm really hurt.'

'Not yet you're not,' Beyonton replied.

'Nobody's accusing you, Ralphy,' Reid grunted, 'and far from it. All right, you have Harpur and even Iles up here, but I know you're no talker. You'd despise that.'

Now and then when Ember had one of his panics, he felt as if his scar had opened again after all these years and was trailing nerve-ends. He put up a hand and touched it.

'Anyway, fireproof or not, we talk to one another only, now, just the three of us, nobody else,' Beyonton said. 'Too many whispers.'

'Ralphy would like a piece of the action, I know it,' Deloraine said. 'And he's been thinking a lot about Kenward's outfit, haven't you, Ralph?'

'No, no,' Ember said. 'Only what I read in the press.'

'Kenward was big, even by your standards, Ralph,' Beyonton said.

'I don't really know much about him,' Ember replied. 'He came on fast, that's all.'

'Finished faster,' Beyonton said.

'Well, drive carefully, lads,' Charles Couzel said. He and the other lawyers were leaving and came in a happy group to the bar. They had a steady glow about them which lawyers radiated sometimes when aware they had pulled off a victory for fair play and justice.

'I'm going to send you a present, Charlie,' Beyonton said. 'I mean, on top of that fucking extortionate fee you're in for anyway, bastard. But seriously, you were a star, and that judge respects you, which is a real clever flair. I was thinking of one of those gold chains with a medallion based on a saint for you, a real saint, not some soccer player or tit-and-bum girl. This would have taste,

15

don't worry. I don't mean wear it in court or down Lincoln's Inn banquets, for God's sake. But when you're on your holidays in a leisure shirt, the Caribbean or Mexico, or wherever you loaded, smart-arse sods go. This would give a genuine glint in the continuous sunshine and make you remember Claud and friends. Just watch you're not mugged for it out there, people like that. Make a change for a lawyer to get mugged instead of mugging the rest of us. But you're still a true star, Charlie.'

The three of them shook hands with the lawyers. 'We won't be needing you again, boys and girls,' Gerry said. He had reclaimed the magnum and handed it around for farewell swigs.

'Of course you won't,' Charles Couzel said. 'You're boys who wanted above all to keep out of trouble but were landed in it by innuendo and lies.'

'Plus, we've got those two dead now,' Harry replied.

Couzel looked shocked and appalled.

'He doesn't mean *those* two, not Alby Horton and McCallion, do you, Harry?' Beyonton said. 'He's talking about Harpur and Iles, that's all. Meaning they're finished after this. Metaphorical?'

Chapter 4

Harpur and Denise were naked and talkative behind the settee on the floor in his big living room, when he thought he heard someone tapping a window very gently – not this room, possibly the kitchen or breakfast cubby-hole at the back. It was clear Denise had not heard, and he felt a bit ashamed to have noticed it himself, as though not rapt by the sweet urgencies and chat of the moment. 'Oh, in due course screw me sweetly, ceaselessly, Col,' Denise chortled, in that heartening, educated voice. 'Let's shake all her damn books from the shelves.'

He greatly liked good, explicit, spoken menus in love-making, impossible or not, and certainly preferred it to the sound of that tapping, whoever it might be. His daughters were in Wales on a judo course, so he did not have to worry about them, and for now was not going to worry about anyone else.

'You could bite me,' she said.

'Are you sure?' He took her nipple in his mouth and found it as warm and pushy as ever. It would be wasted on babies.

'Well, not right through. With delicacy. Both.'

After a while, when that had finished, he said: 'You could bite me.'

'Are you sure?'

'Not right through. With delicacy. Just the one.' He knew he would be warm and allowed himself to be pushy, too, though not injuriously.

She drew away from him suddenly with a fine slurping sound. 'I hear tapping,' she said.

'Sod that. A night woodpecker.'

'Col, what is it? I mean, to find us like this, entwined and floorboarded in your own home.'

'Just forget it,' he said and nuzzled her again.

'Well, all right,' she said.

'Stop talking now.'

'Col,' she said, hesitantly, 'just tell me this, all right? Now, don't get shirty. Well, did you ever do this before?'

'What?'

'Make love among the cobwebs here with – with your wife.'

He knew she disliked using Megan's name. 'Here? Why would I?' he said.

'Oh, it could have been, like, an impulse – something wild. Although married. God, how I hate to think of that.'

'Don't.'

'What do you mean, don't think of it because it didn't happen, or don't think of it because it did? I loathe your past. It doesn't belong to me.'

'There wasn't much to things between Megan and me by the time she died – was killed. Over. She was looking elsewhere.'

This was the first time he had ever been able to persuade Denise into his house, or, as she would call it, his own home, although he had been single for months, a genuine widower. The three-day absence of the children was decisive. She still drew the line at his double bed, though. He found such delicacy strange in an independent minded undergraduate of nearly twenty. Perhaps what people said was right; today's students had turned sensitive.

They lay looked down on by Megan's books, which he and his daughters definitely meant to get rid of one day, definitely one day soon. For Denise, the books obviously screamed Megan, like the bedroom. For Harpur, too, the books screamed Megan, so should he keep them or let them go? The lights were off. Denise and Harpur both felt it would be gross to make love on a living room, library, floor except in the dark.

'I adore it – you,' she said.

'Right order.'

'Just shut up,' she said. 'Oh, Col, love me. Love me hard, harder.'

'God, the young – so exorbitant.'

'Needy.'

There were times when Harpur felt Denise was too beautiful for screwing, and especially screwing in the kind of unkempt locales they had to use, like this chill corner of the room among a decade's debris. Always he managed to triumph over these scruples, but they were another reason for keeping the lights out now: he could not see her gorgeous face, and worked around her gorgeous body by, he hoped, reverent touch. He had first met her via the girlfriend of one of his prime informants, and still marvelled that police work could produce such a lovely source of joy.

They sat up afterwards and leaned against the back of the settee. She had what felt like an ancient parking-ticket stuck to her thigh, and he peeled it off. 'I'm going to discover who's out there,' he said. The noise continued intermittently. He hunted clothes.

'Another woman? Her turn?' she asked.

'Probably. Where's my diary?'

'Swine. I wish I'd bitten rougher. Ownership marks.'

He pulled on trousers and a sweater.

'It could be dangerous,' she said.

'Dangerous people don't knock the window.'

'You sure?'

'No. I'll take a fire iron. I'll be formidable.' He recalled his daughters arming themselves like that one day when they thought an intruder was in the garden.

'An iron for me? I should come with you.'

19

'No, just get dressed,' he whispered. 'I might have to let someone in. You look unambiguous.'

'Who says it's only one?'

'Nobody.'

'So I ought to come with you.'

'Dress and stand by the phone, love. I won't be in trouble but if it sounds as if I could be, just do nine-nine-nine straight away. My name will be enough. It's Harpur. Say you're the butler.'

'Oh, stop being so bloody mature and cool.'

'Dismally mature. Not cool. Then get out of here. Anywhere.'

'Leave you to it?'

'Help will come.'

'I'm help.'

'Just get out, Denise.'

She looked full of wild, teenage rage and astonishment, plus some hurt. 'Do you think I would, Col? *Could I*, for God's sake? Is that how you see me? If it was Megan, would you tell her to ditch you, too?'

'Just don't hang about,' he replied.

'Ashamed to have them find me in your home?'

He picked up the poker and went into the kitchen, keeping against the wall, a bit crouched, very obvious. He wore no shoes or socks and was reasonably quiet. He still did without lights. An acquittal or a case-collapse made people think they could never be touched again, and they might be right. They forgot about risk, went out stalking those who had menaced them. Beyonton could be like that, and Harry Foster. Beyonton had the face of a decent little mouse, but more ferocity. Perhaps even that dreaming spiel king, Gerry Reid, could turn brutal. After all, that dreaming spiel king had done his share in getting rid of Albert Horton and McCallion. The information put him very much at the scene and active. All right, an old wig said the information did not rate, but old wigs were frightened now by all the mistakes they'd made in the

20

past. From Sunday-school days Harpur remembered a text, *Judge not that ye be not judged*. They had fallen for that one.

As he stood near the kitchen door, he saw a hand appear outside from beneath the window, a hand in a black woollen mitten, and with a bit of sleeve also visible, like a puppeteer with no puppet, or someone dying in a trench. The thumb and forefinger held a ten-pence piece, and this was used to tap the window, four lots of three smart knocks, as though it was some known code, the way prisoners talked on jail heating pipes. Harpur's education did not cover this as yet. He waited for a face, faces to appear.

It was true, dangerous people probably did not tap windows, not unless they wanted to draw someone into the back garden for a look around and whatever. Now and then Claud Beyonton could let hatred run ahead of good business sense. Seeing off Horton and McCallion would have been very good business sense, especially if you got away with it. Seeing off Harpur would be hate only. The effect was identical.

After a few minutes, the hand appeared again and gave the same message. This time the coin looked more prominent. Perhaps the moon had come out, making it seem to radiate the bright, beckoning evil gleam of a bribe. Would people fix this as about Harpur's price if he ever started on the take? What else could he read in this hand, this mitten, this sleeve? Not much to form a profile from, but he did not believe Claud Beyonton would stoop to black woollen mittens, nor stoop under a window and stay stooped and faceless so long in someone's backyard. There was not much sleeve on show. He thought it was some sort of khaki; an imitation combat jacket, which again would be wrong for Beyonton. Although Claud lived by combat, he did not dress for it. Claud liked the formal. Reid, Foster?

Harpur crossed the room and looked down. A face was

staring up, and he recognized it even in the dark. Harpur went to the kitchen door, unbolted and opened it. 'Come in,' he said. 'You'll freeze.'

'Someone with you, yes? I've been watching the house and saw a girl go in, too.'

'It'll be all right.'

'I wouldn't want to meet anyone.'

'It will be all right.'

'And then no lights in the house.'

'I was in bed,' Harpur replied.

'Well, you're entitled.'

Harpur shut the kitchen door and put the poker on the table. 'There's no blind for the window. We're overlooked by a couple of houses. Maybe we should sit in the dark. Do you mind?'

'Some other room?'

'It would be better here,' Harpur said.

'Someone else about?'

'Well, yes.'

'You're entitled, regardless.'

'Yes, thanks. Here's a chair, look. I can make some tea. I know the way around.' He lit a gas ring on the stove, which gave some light, then filled the kettle. 'Hang on here, will you? I'll just tell her I'm busy.' The 999 call would be a mistake. He picked up the poker to take back.

'I'm a nuisance. Will she understand?'

'I'll say it's something urgent,' Harpur replied.

'Yes, it's urgent. Would I come to your house if not?'

Harpur returned to the living room. He could make out Denise sitting near the telephone at what he still thought of as Megan's desk. She had put his suit jacket around her, but had nothing else on. It did him good to think of her bare-arsed on Megan's work chair, another happy advance. 'No need to phone,' he said. He put the poker back in the empty grate. 'A job thing.'

Someone stupid might have said, 'At this hour?', or 'In your own home?', but she was not that, and knew police work had its oddities. 'I thought best not dress yet, after all,' she replied. 'So damn defeatist.'

'It won't take long. Are you warm enough? I'll turn the heat up. Or why don't you go to bed?'

'Oh, you opportunist bastard,' she said.

'He wonders why the house is dark.'

'Do we care if he wonders?' she replied.

'I'll show you the way. Then I could bring him in here and have some lights.'

'Why can't you have lights in the kitchen?'

'No blind.'

'He's someone who mustn't be seen?'

He did not answer that. It seemed on a par with 'In your own home?'

'All right,' she said.

'Good.'

'But I'm not stopping the whole night. Col, not the whole night.' She yelled it the second time, and he glanced towards the kitchen. 'Not breakfast.'

'Understood.'

'My clothes are all around the place.'

'I'll clear up before I bring him in.'

He took her upstairs into the bedroom and put the light on there. She hesitated for a moment, gazing about. There was still some of Megan's make-up stuff on the dressing table, and some of her clothes showing in an open wardrobe. A couple of framed holiday photographs of her and Harpur, looking full of happiness and affection, stood on the mantelpiece. 'I don't know if I can, Col,' Denise said. The voice was like a child's. He lifted a pubic hair off her lip.

Leaving her in the doorway, he went and turned down the cover. 'I'm scrupulous about clean sheets – every six weeks, or even less, say five and a half,' he told her. 'You don't have to worry.'

She edged forward, eyes half closed as though wanting to ignore the room, and then rolled suddenly into the bed, still wearing his jacket. He switched off the light and went back downstairs. To know she was in the big bed made him feel secure and almost familial, especially as he would be holding all her clothes, so she could not secretly do a runner. Switching the lights on in the living room, he tidied up, bundling her things together quickly and shoving them into the drinks cupboard. The curtains in this room did not quite close in the middle, but he pulled them across as far as they would go and then went back to the kitchen. The kettle was boiling and he filled the teapot and prepared a tray. He led the way back to the living room. 'I'm going to put the lights on,' he said. 'Just keep to this side of the room. We're not visible from outside, unless someone comes right up and sticks his face against the window.'

'Who says they won't?'

'Only the back of your head, anyway, if you sit here.' Harpur switched on.

'Wasn't Josh McCallion hit in the back of the head?'

'Just heart.'

'Listen, Mr Harpur, don't think I'm not grateful, very grateful, but I'm scared now.'

'I know. We'll work something out. I was going to be in touch, but one thing and the other, Keith.'

'Well, lucky.' He glanced up to the ceiling and the bedroom, then sucked some tea. He was holding the mug with two hands, still wearing the mittens. 'I wouldn't mind something in this.'

'Sure.' Harpur went to the drinks cupboard. When he opened the door, Denise's knickers and jeans fell out on to the carpet. He had to pick up the two items separately, and replaced them in the cupboard. He took a bottle of whisky to top up both cups. Harpur had a nurtured fetish about her knickers, only hers: why he had hurriedly wrapped everything into a general parcel before, so as not to grow light-headed. Now, his hand shook as he poured the whisky.

24

Keith probably noticed but did not comment. 'I could disappear, Mr Harpur. Or I could stay around, play innocent, ignorant.'

'We need to discuss.'

'Why I'm here. Christ, that judge, though. I got it from the paper.' He took off one glove and brought a clipping out of his jacket pocket. He read: *'In the absence of the informant or informants used by the police, the court cannot know whether this informant or these informants were themselves part of the illegal drug trade in this city, and therefore interested parties in the deaths and in these prosecutions and deeply unreliable.'* This is so harsh, Mr Harpur, the clever bugger.'

'It's happening all the time, Keith,' Harpur said. 'This was him trying to squeeze me. My last chance before he pulled the plug.'

'Well, thanks anyway. Silence.'

'I promised you, Keith.'

'Police often promise.'

'We don't blow sources.'

'The cost of it – lawyers, everything.'

'We don't blow sources or there won't be any.'

'What use are they anyway, now?'

Fair enough.

'If I disappear, they look around and see who's missing. I hear of tipsters hit by contract even gone abroad. New life, new name, lederhosen, everything, but still hit. Even Madrid.' His voice was flat, a real piece of control, though his eyes over the rim of the mug looked sick and empty.

'Press scare-stories, Keith.'

'If I stay – well, if I stay . . .' He raised his gaze from the mug to the bedroom again. 'You busy, quite tied up, Mr Harpur, and no time to look after the likes of Keith Vine. Claud – he can work things out, even if I don't leave. That little mouse-face and mousey smell, but there's a foxy brain there. Plus bloody Harry.'

Yes, his voice was flat but it had a note in it that seemed

25

to say he had been betrayed somehow, slandering fink, jerk. Harpur wished he knew him better, could read him better, but Vine was not a grass he had ever used before. The judge in his rancid, programmed way probably had him right: Keith was drugs turned grass because he had wanted Claud and Harry and Gerry Reid out of the way on a life sentence, and a clearer path to Kenward Knapp's empire. The press clichéd on and on about the 'code of silence' in the drugs game. And there was one. Ask Manchester, Moss Side police. But it could be dropped if someone like Keith saw possible business gain in a little well-placed conversation. You did not sell people for money, but a career move was something else. Keith had not asked for a grass's fee. Everyone struggled after one thing only, that smoothed-out path to Kenward's coke and Ecstasy empire and a lasting, glorious future. This was how the whole thing started, with Horton and McCallion. They had wanted a slice, too. See it as a family fight over the famed, fat estate. Yes, a clever bugger to read the situation, that judge.

'We can help you if you run,' Harpur said. 'What I mean is, we can help you if you stay, too – keep an eye, within reason. It would be crazy to make the guard too obvious, or people like Claud soon work out what it means. But if you run and need setting up somewhere as new, there are very quiet official funds for that. Housing, travel, furniture. Abroad. Anywhere. We can do an identity for you and yours – your girl, that is – passport, National Insurance, library tickets, no trouble. I'll miss you, Keith.'

'A lot of people in the know.'

'They're secure, believe me. They prize you. We depend on your sort.'

'Yes?'

'It's been done before. We've got a procedure.'

'I've heard.'

'It works.'

'Yes?' He drank with real energy, like someone rescued from the desert. 'I might stay.' He twitched inside the combat jacket, as if pulling himself together, toughening himself for a fight, dismissing the notion of retreat. He was burly enough, filled the bogus uniform well, and had a good square, big-chinned, heavy-duty face. The telly used to show troops like this, road-patrolling in Northern Ireland. He was about twenty-five, fair hair cropped right down, wide-necked, wide-shouldered, thin-waisted. It seemed the wrong sort of face and physique to cower in a back garden, making help-me-do signals with a coin – as wrong as for Beyonton. In the ring, Keith would eat Claud. That's not where they might meet, though.

Harpur could watch Vine do the usual actuarial calculations for his sort of spot. As he said, if he baled out people would notice and he might be traced. There were professionals for such work, contracted, ready to travel. Also, if he baled out he lost any chance of the Knapp carve-up, and all the risk-taking would be worth nothing. Untenanted domains like Kenward's were rare, and Keith probably had as much greed and bright ambition in him as any other operator. These stopped his face from becoming lifeless and slabby. Dangers could look smaller when viewed against the prospect of endless, grand street cash collections. On the other hand, if he stayed, it was perilous, perilous, perilous, but at least he knew the geography here, and the people and the trade possibilities, and at least there was Harpur to remember a debt and do occasional protection, when he decided to pull his head out from between a pair of welcoming young legs. Or if.

'Well, I won't keep you, Mr Harpur. You've earned your full life, no gainsaying. My worries are mine.'

They were Harpur's, too. 'Look, I'll be in touch, Keith. A two-word phone call to name a meeting spot.'

'Like, *Don't call me, I'll call you.*'

'Call me whenever you want. I just thought it would be better the other way.'

27

He stood. 'Well, you might have some hazard yourself, you know, Mr Harpur. They don't like being buggered about, even if acquitted. This address – in the phone book, for God's sake. Secure?'

'Oh, I see no problem there, Keith. That would be stupid of them.'

'Yes? But not stupid to go for me.'

'Yes, that would be stupid, too. We'll make it stupid.'

When Harpur went to the bedroom, Denise had fallen asleep. This was one of those problems that could be easily solved, though, not like Keith's difficulties.

Chapter 5

Harpur said, 'He *is* our man, sir.'

'We do have obligations, Chief,' Iles said. 'If he wishes to stay.'

'Of course he's our man, and of course we have obligations,' Lane replied. 'He gave traceable tips, trying to help us. He took appalling risks. He was clearly in the category of "protected informant" – one who grasses on colleagues and is not prosecuted. If he *had* been prosecuted, I'd have approved putting in a so-called "Text" to court, confidentially detailing his help to us and requesting leniency. And now – well, now, I'm ready to provide funds to move him and his to wherever he wishes, this country, abroad – every expense paid. All that's routine. But if he wants to remain here, he's on his own. And Col tells us he does.' Lane spoke the special terms and their meanings mockingly, contemptuously – as if they were black magic curses.

'Some of them hate being uprooted, sir,' Harpur replied. 'It's understandable. Their community. And people have been hit even after moving.'

'Community?' Lane replied. 'Keith Vine wants the Kenward Knapp leavings. That's what keeps him here, not love for the old folks at home. Am I supposed to protect people trading coke and Ecstasy on my own manor, for God's sake? What kind of alliance is that? What kind of policing?'

The questions asked what they asked. Harpur saw they

said something beyond that, though. They said Lane still wondered if Iles and Harpur knew more than they showed, knew it as insiders, as kickback profit-takers. It was the Chief's obsession, poor sod, perhaps all Chiefs' obsessions about their people. But in Lane it was central, and at times like this he screamed pathetically from his eternal plagued, honest isolation.

'We could have another death, sir, or other deaths,' Harpur said. 'These three ran wild even before the acquittals.'

Lane sat back suddenly like a victorious Boat Race cox and began to shout. 'I tell you, this is exactly the hellish spread of evil that comes from our dependence on informants in the first place. We are dragged into we don't know what. No Controller – and therefore no control, I mean generally.' The three of them were at the big conference table in his office, Lane wearing a quite decent beigeish suit and good, silver-dotted tie. Beige was his colour. This smartness and the formal shape of the meeting were unusual. Lane generally went after casualness in dress and discussions. He must be determined to impose himself today, wag rank at them. Two all-out wars were under way on this patch. The drugs teams fought one another for Kenward's inheritance. And Lane battled with his top people for power. Keith Vine and any close to him might get slaughtered in the crossfire.

The Chief quietened a little and went deep. 'Yes, I have to side with the judge in the Horton McCallion case. All right, it appears a defeat for us, a terrible rout of law and order. But he was only too correct to demand our informant should be subjected to the rigours of the court.'

'Naturally, I'm having urgent, private inquiries made about that fucking his Honour, sir,' Iles replied. 'See if we can get something on him to interest the tabloids. There has to be dirt. You don't get lips like that sucking ice lollies.'

Lane said: 'I seek positives and—'

'Why you're so justifiably at our head, sir,' Iles replied. 'Positives are leadership.'

Lane said: 'And what I like to think is that such failed cases will ultimately bring the end of policing by informants. We can get back to proving our cases through proper, honest witnesses.'

'Jesus Christ,' Iles replied.

The Chief said: 'We shall be freed from—'

'In drug wars there are no witnesses,' Iles said. 'None, never mind proper and honest. They're all scared shitless and silent. Or bought off. It's so bad, they've got a witness protection scheme in Greater Manchester. We've had that Lord Chancellor's committee looking at ways to keep witnesses in one piece long enough to testify.'

Lane tilted his wan face towards the ceiling and beyond, a message for the heavens as well as for all below. 'I will not have intimidation here,' the Chief hissed. 'Policing cannot function without the aid of the populace. People must be made to feel they should help us, and can help us, free from risk. *Free from risk*. To achieve this is one of my prime aims.' He stared at Iles. Those thin red lines of excitement and sacred mission which sometimes broke through gleamed in Lane's cheeks. 'But you, Desmond – you cannot really believe we should encourage this grass to stay, and offer him protection.'

'Yes, I'd say so,' Iles replied. 'The more of them here picking over Kenward's proud bones, the more chance they'll kill one another. I like that. They do our job. We pull the protection off at the due moment. Seconds out!'

Lane formed his face into something near resolution. 'This is a police force, for God's sake. We do not incite murder.'

'How else to get them now if judges have gone to the enemy?' Iles asked. But he drew out his notebook and made a parade of writing, *We do not incite murder*.

When they left Lane, the ACC came down to Harpur's room. 'That man – a gem, Col,' Iles said. 'You won't meet

31

many like that, no matter how high you go in the service, as if you were going higher. I don't know what pills they've been feeding him, but his illness and the lay-off have gravely reconstituted all his fine, fart-arseing principles from fairyland. Is he a cop or a *Guardian* leader writer, the sad, dear, anxious twat?'

All Iles's questions required answers. 'Perhaps he's adapting faster than us to new policing conditions, sir.'

'Perceptive as ever, Col. Well, the wet sod can adapt on his own, Harpur. You'd let the courts trample you, that backscratching, coining clique?'

'Well, sir, we—'

'I know Col Harpur better than that, I think. Terrorized by a dead-beat trendy wig and some bought-and-sold QC? Never.'

'Well, sir, we—'

'Good boy, Col. One thing I've asked my investigative people to look at is if his judgeship and Charlie Couzel QC are a loving couple. I thought I noticed a *tendresse*. Inns of Court run on it. Their code for buggery is "eating dinners". So, a judge squeaks, Lane collapses. Such gut-lessness is clearly basic for promotion to Chief, yet I'll make it one day, don't worry, and there might be a job for you with me.' He pondered that. 'I don't know, though. That stuff about the holy "structure" for handling grasses! He was a passable detective himself once, wasn't he, Harpur?'

'Much better than that.'

'So he ought to recall that the most basic skill in the game is how to skirt such "structures", shouldn't he?'

'Well, sir—'

'What we've got in your grass is a unique piece of bait, wouldn't you say, Harpur?'

'Well, sir—'

'I like your phrase "the new policing". You always were a wordsmith. How do you see it, Harpur, "the new policing"?'

'Well, sir—'

'The detective is dead.'

'Sir? Which detective? I hadn't heard.'

'Jerk. The detective as species.' Iles pushed three straight-backed chairs together and lay out on them, still as a corpse, arms folded across his chest. He wore a brilliantly white, handmade shirt, and the thin-legged trousers of a grey flannel suit. His shoes were slim, black slip-ons and his motif tie might indicate a rugby club or some Masonic special committee. The ACC had his eyes closed. 'Courts won't hear confessions, they throw out informant cases, still give every career villain the right to silence, disbelieve police evidence as a matter of course. Judges disallow material recorded in trap situations – alleging we're *provocateurs*. Juries are threatened and bribed. Villains keep special insurance funds for nobbling them. Where's detection? How do we prove anything, Col?'

'Well, sir—'

'We don't. From now on, we need to catch the sods at it. Given luck, we catch them at it when there's gunplay, so we can shoot too, and knock them over. No trial rigmarole. No QC smarm-bucket with his, "If you please, Detective Chief Superintendent, and no My Lord lording it and playing the libertarian." Or with even more luck, if it's gang stuff, they'll knock one another over. All we have to do is the official count, notify relatives, and comfort any bereaved pussy that's pretty and looks halfway clean. This is why your lad is so valuable, Col. He's going to draw Beyonton and co. like Cynthia draws the sea. And we're waiting there.'

'Which Cynthia is that, sir? This some artist?'

'The fucking moon, Harpur. Did you ever get to school?'

'The Chief says we're not to give protection if he stays put, sir.'

'This is not quite protection, Harpur. No. This is making

33

an offering of him. He's volunteered for it.'

'Sir, he tried to help us.'

'He tried to help himself.'

'That's what grassing is about. Quid pro quo.'

Iles opened an eye, disturbing in a cadaver, even a mock one. 'You streetwise old devil, Col. But thanks so very much for the lesson. Well, he might come through it.'

Harpur said: 'If the Chief won't allow protection he won't allow that kind of surveillance, either.'

Iles sat up, both eyes open. 'I love the Chief, revere him. Do I need to say?'

'Quite, sir,' Harpur replied.

'This is a prized leader, Col, who must be allowed to go his own treacherous, addled way towards beatification, while policing in this domain is done by those who know how things work. Perhaps I've mentioned to you before a line from George Savile's *The Character of a Trimmer*, seventeenth century?'

'Is this, *There was a young lady from Split
Famous for*—?'

'He says the laws have to be "in good hands", Harpur. That's me. Maybe you. Obviously never Lane, and not that wanking wig. You've got some good boys?'

'Our best surveillance man is dead, sir.'

'Ah, the great Erogenous Jones, yes. No successors?'

'One or two.'

'I knew it. You'll probably want to do an occasional stint yourself, Col.'

'Will I, sir?'

'You value your tipster, don't you?'

'Like you said, sir, I feel an obligation.'

'Same thing. I'd like to be on the spot there myself now and then with a happy Bulldog Magnum. But it's not seemly at my rank. Bishops hate an ACC smelling of cordite at civic functions.'

'Of course, Vine might change his mind and decide to move after all.'

'You talk him into that, Harpur, or fail to talk him out of it, and you're ashes. Understand?'

'Well, sir—'

'If you can find an excuse, arm the people who watch him. Something that makes big, ragged, untourniquetable holes.'

Chapter 6

Keith Vine had two thoughts. One was a gun. He knew guns and loved them, their look and weight and feel, their mechanical sweetness, the unmistakable little messages they carried. He decided he needed one now, if he stayed. He had a lot to look after, and there would be more.

But his other big thought was he should not stay after all. He had told Harpur he would, but that was to shock the smug sod, show him Keith Vine was not a lad to be parcelled up and express-posted somewhere far and forgettable. It had angered him, the way Harpur continued with his fine, juicy life while everything around slid to hell. They were like that. For them, the disaster and perils were just work, and they went home after shift and did their garden or young talent.

So, maybe write off Kenward's inheritance and make a move, perhaps abroad. It could be stupid to turn down all the police help, so different from what they usually offered. Milk them. They would be putting out a hundred grand, for God's sake. And Kenward's inheritance was full of possible grief, on top of the possible grief he already had from the trial.

He glanced around the flat's small living room, with its glued three-ply furniture and the second-hand, ciggy-scarred TV. What was so great about being here? He liked the sound of France, and so did Becky. She spoke the word France with full, reverent breath, like it was some magic spot where all you did was water the lawn and spread pâté in the shade. They had talked about France over and over. Becky felt some warm part in the South would be great to bring up a baby in, when it arrived mid-June. She said it would be useful for a child to have two languages from birth, a real advantage because of the EU, boy or girl. They could be content out there, new all through. Also, she most likely thought she would have a good chance of keeping hold of him if they were strangers in some foreign country, so much more tied to each other. Now they had the kid on the way, that sort of thinking was natural. He understood, and did not really blame her.

But then the doubts came back, this mighty feeling of waste. 'Christ, can I ditch a great business chance here, Becky? I think about that. A child has needs. I look at people like Panicking Ralph who's lived right on the edge for ever, yet he's hung on and piled it up quietly, kids at private school, gymkhanas, no stinting. Things go all right, we could afford a better place.'

'You'd do fine wherever, Keith.' She had this big-eyed way of buttering when she wanted something.

'Strange country, strange ways. Would I find partners?' he said. 'I can't operate alone.'

'Maybe you wouldn't need so much business, anyway. I mean, we'd have the house, all paid for.'

'No kid of mine will be poor. I've been through that.' He never had, really, not anything like poverty, but it gave him a kick to say this sort of thing, like those working-class MPs. He loved sounding as though he had a big purpose and theme, was not just drifting from one rough outing to the next.

'Some little, ordinary job could be enough, Keith. Cheap fruit, a climate with low fuel bills.'

Probably she was right. This enraged him. Was that what she thought about Keith Vine, that he would fit into some little, ordinary job? Did he look like some little, ordinary job? If he had wanted some little, ordinary job

37

he could have had one in this country a long time ago. What was some little, ordinary job in France – degriming a château swimming pool, sawdusting a horse butcher's floors? Did she want this child's father in some little, ordinary French job? His own father had been in some little, ordinary job, and hers as well, every illness National Health. He needed progress, for God's sake. But he did not show any anger. That would be stupid. Play along until the perfect moment.

'I owe it to Alby Horton and McCallion,' he said and gave this good weight. She gazed at him. He knew she would try to work out how to answer, in a way respectful to Alby and Josh, but which killed the argument.

Keith thought a gun was a bright idea whether they left or not. He would feel bigger. They could be around here for a while, anyway, waiting for arrangements, and if Claud got a whisper that might be danger time. Even if they did go, he still needed to be ready for awkward visitors arriving suddenly one warm night at their remote, vine-clad villa. Nowhere was safe now. He would not say that to Becky. She had enough to bother her. Probably she understood, anyway.

She said, 'They were good friends, I know, Keith. But they're dead. We can't run our lives for them, can we, love?

'We were going to be a great business, the three of us. We'd have taken Kenward's operation, or a fair piece. I still say I must carry on for Alby and Josh's sake.'

'Great thought, Keith, but you tried to do something for them. That was the trial, the talking to police.'

'The only reason I would ever do it – to put things right for friends.'

'I know that.'

'I'm no grass. Not grassing just for the sake of it, or loot. This was a debt to be paid.' He pushed his chin out. He had integrity and fight.

There was a lad called Leyton Harbinger who did weaponry, sale or hire. To Leyton, guns were business only, and he had no real love of them, no feel, but Keith did not mind dealing with him because he always came up with what he said he would come up with, and the pieces were always in beautiful order. Obviously, you did not call on him at home, but everyone knew his pub, The Hobart, and you just hung about and waited, or someone would give him a call if you asked at the bar, and you looked all right. They had a parrot there, but not a talker. Leyton stayed out of the phone book. Leyton kept busy.

Becky said: 'I know you're no career grass, darling. But they're not going to look at it that way, no question, people like Claud Beyonton. Why we've got to get clear. Those people wipe out two partners. You're next, especially now.'

Most likely she was right, again. She had a brain in there, Becky. This was a girl of real worth. She had quite a body even now the kid had started, and it would probably be fully recoverable eventually, plus good, nearly blonde hair, and skin as fresh as you could expect with worldwide pollution. Although her green eyes looked nice and sleepy when she was not giving some flattery, they saw a lot and maybe too much. She had presence. Harpur would belt anything teenage to twenty-three, but many people preferred some loyalty, something solid in these friendless times approaching the twenty-first century. 'I'm really going to think about this,' he told her. 'I'll try to see it from your point of view, love.'

'And it's yours, Keith. Plus our child's.'

That stoked up his rage a lot more. She was using this baby to put the pressure on him, the smart way they had. A woman would never understand the sort of comrade debt he felt to Alby and Josh. Probably those two fumblers would have been useless going for Kenward's operation, but they were his partners all the same. To her they would be just two deads, and he was just someone lucky not to be with them. She could be right on that, as well.

He smiled at Becky wombwards and nodded lovingly.

Mostly, people dealing with Leyton Harbinger hired. They did not want a gun around after an outing. But he would sell, also. He had his suppliers, which you never asked about, naturally, and Keith had heard since the Berlin Wall went down a lot of his guns came from East Europe. That was all right. They had a prime tradition over there because of plentiful wars. Most people thought of that Wall as politics, but there was also this handgun side to it. Keith needed the fire-power long term, not just for one outing like most of Leyton's clients, so he would have to buy, not hire. Buying meant four to five hundred for something decent and new, though, and he did not have that kind of money for the moment. What he thought was, a few days' hire at first, and try a collection with it somewhere, a shop or post office. Then he should have enough to buy, and for that kind of deal Leyton would usually knock half the hire fee off the sell price. He was a sound, kindly lad, Leyton, not greedy, wanting his clients to keep coming back again unless they got blasted, but what you did not do was pay to hire and then keep it. Leyton had a nice organization and it would track you. Not Leyton himself, but staff, and they would be armed with the best, naturally. Keith had enough folk hunting him.

'Give me a while, then, Becky,' he said.

'How long?'

Obviously, she thought she had him on the run, she was really pushing. But still he did not show anger.

'It's not safe,' she said, and touched the baby-lump. 'That Reid, half mad, thinking they're indestructible now.'

'Not long, I promise. And I'll do a few inquiries about France. I know a lad who worked there.'

'Worked?'

'Had some really good business going there.'

'Business?'

'Successful.'

'Why's he back?'

'I'll talk to him. I'll go and see him now.'

'Is this Stan Stanfield?' she asked. 'He was in France, wasn't he? Came home empty.'

'Yes, Stan. He saw better chances here, what I mean. He can judge a situation.'

'Don't say too much, Keith. Talk travels.'

'Stan's all right.'

'All the same.'

Stan could wait. When Keith reached The Hobart he found he was frightened to go in and kept walking. The worry was the tale could be around about who put Claud Beyonton and the others on trial, and even though not many loved dear Claud they would love a tipster much less. Like Becky said, people did not want to understand about leaking for Alby's and Josh's sake. To them in their crude thinking an informant was an informant was a fink. Leyton would not deal with a grass. That would be a principle, but also, if he had heard about Keith and the case he would guess what the gun was for and could not afford to be pulled into a battle with Claud and the others as caterer to their talkie target.

Keith walked on and came out into Cork Street, a wide through-road, plenty of cars and people, a real hum. All that activity made him feel better suddenly, stronger. This was a good, busy city, with plenty of chances if you knew how to do it, and how to do it was not about getting scared to walk into some pub. He was Keith Vine, Keith Vine, Keith Vine. He would take over from Kenward Knapp. He had a kid coming to think of and a girl who believed in him. All right, she wanted France, but he was sure she would change when he explained the scale of what Kenward had left and showed her a fine pistol. If he did things right and kept an eye open and a gun handy, some of the drivers and pedestrians bustling about here in Cork Street would be buying stuff from him soon, desperate for the product. This business had said nuts to the slump. That's what made it so beautiful. What people could not cut down on was a habit.

Keith turned around and went back to The Hobart, straight in this time, no creeping past. He felt bigger already. People here would see right off he was a serious element. This was not someone to dodge overseas and get anonymous. This was Keith Vine, Keith Vine, Keith Vine. He had roots. He had a future.

He had a past, too, and Harbinger would remember him. Keith had hired twice before. He had not needed to fire either time, but he could tell the weapons were good and not too old, just from the look and smell. This was the trouble with hiring, you never knew if you were getting a gun that had done active service. Of course, armourers always said this would never happen, and if a weapon had been used they would get rid. Did they, though? That was costly. How could they know, anyway, whether a gun had been fired on a job or only for practice? So, you could get something matchable by Ballistics to an event, or even events, that would lock you up for ever if you were caught with it. You returned hired weapons fast. That risk was for the armourer, in the fee.

Once you were inside a pub like The Hobart you felt even better, because you could tell it was the sort of place you belonged. Same as Ralph Ember's place, the Monty. People would give you a quick look in case you were law or some slumming fart from up town, and then, when they decided no problem, they would forget you. Keith fitted in here. This would not be true in Marseilles, for instance, or even Cannes. Roots. Naturally, Keith had the old antennae out now, trying to pick up whether they knew the grass story and had a grudge. You would see the faces go stone and someone might move to the door to make sure you did not leave early. But he did not notice anything like that. He was in, he was part of it, as ever.

'Well, here's young Keith,' Leyton bellowed. 'I hear a

babbie on the stocks. This deserves a good drink. How about you call him after me, Keith, or Leytonella if a girl? Myself and Amy, sadly childless. Yes.'

Leyton was with Amy at a table, and she put a hand over his, next to the tankard. They were a good couple, mostly full of giggles and plans, but sad for a minute. Keith had met Amy last time and she usually held the money and counted it, counted it right out in front of you and as soon as you paid, so you could see it was aboveboard. That's how they both were, absolutely no fancy work, unless you turned difficult yourself. Leyton bought some more beers and they toasted the baby. 'So, this call is business, yes, Keith? You're feeling these new responsibilities and need to move the career along?'

Amy had one of her laughs. 'Pity you weren't around here twenty years ago. Maybe you could have helped us out on the baby stakes, Keith. I think I could have enjoyed that.'

She was past it now, thank God, knocking fifty, but still neat and keeping the sag more or less back. Keith said: 'Well, I'm looking for something short term first, but then moving on to a purchase of a new model, Leyton. Something with a good magazine.'

'We see some lovely stuff these days,' Amy said. 'Not recent manufacture but unused, warehoused for years I suppose, and with the nice character they could give pistols in the sixties, seventies.'

'She's like you, Keith. Are they works of art? There's a Russian job.'

'This is the Makarov SL, 9 mm,' Amy said.

'I've heard of it,' Keith replied. 'Like the Walther PP.'

'Right,' Amy said, 'but a spring magazine catch.'

'Eight rounds,' Keith said.

'You need more?' she asked. 'Who you expecting, hordes?'

'Eight's fine.'

'This is four-fifty to buy, with thirty rounds,' Leyton

said. 'If this gun is an investment, you don't want to go less than thirty.'

'Right.'

'Hiring, we've been doing the Smith and Wesson 645,' Amy told him. 'This is a real frightener. As I remember, you'd rather have automatics, not revolvers.'

'Just the look – less cowboy, more city. Keith Vine's image.'

'This is a .45,' Leyton said. 'I've got one never been shot at all, as far as I know. It's been out, but virgin, not even for practice. So it's on no computer. This is a hundred a twenty-four hour day, Keith.'

'Have you got the outing planned, timed?' Amy asked.

'Not yet.'

'Do that first, so you don't need to over-hire,' she replied. 'You don't want it more than two days.' This was like her, not grasping, a nurse's voice, concerned about you and costs. 'Leyton will reserve it, now we know. You're going after the money for the Makarov? Don't look surprised. People are doing it all the time. We can take off at least one of the hire hundreds, can't we Leyton?'

'To a pregnant dad? Of course.'

Keith bought some more beers. It seemed obvious no whisper was around.

Although The Hobart was like the Monty in some ways, it did not have the style of Ralph Ember's place, but Keith liked it better. Or anyway, he liked it better now, because there was quick friendship from Leyton and Amy, and in The Hobart if Leyton and Amy said OK most would smile and try to trust you; they were royalty here. Keith soon felt he was not offering his life. OK, Ember's club had all that mahogany and brass, but what could you do with them? Amy said: 'Come in later when you've got a date and we'll finalize. Nothing too obvious. Well, you'll remember. The landlord's understanding. Understands too fucking much.'

'He'd never talk,' Leyton said, 'but we *are* careful.'

'Nobody knows who'll talk if the situation's right,' Amy replied.

She did not look at Keith, though, even for a second, he felt sure. 'It's sickening,' he replied.

'Some, never,' Leyton said.

'I believe it,' Keith replied.

'We've got to believe it, or where are we?' Leyton stated. 'The whole structure would break apart.' He gazed slowly around The Hobart like this was the world, and worth conservation. It was a huge square, scruffy pub, basic décor, the parrot in its tall cage, and walls full of boxing homage pictures and bout bills going back to Marciano. You could see what they meant about Harpur looking like him, but fair. 'There are folk here now, splendid parents, really ordinary, fine folk – boys and girls, Keith, who would kill a grass like routine,' Leyton said.

'Ultimately, people look after their corner, that's all,' Amy replied. 'If talking seems long-term profitable they'll talk.'

'No, no,' Leyton groaned. 'We can't have that, can we, Keith? It would be sick.' He was about forty, and let his fair hair pile up in curls. It made him look like the headmaster's pet. People said Leyt needed someone older and maybe brighter, such as Amy, because outside his trade and this pub he was a lost boy. You could not run a full life on curls. A lot of men were hopeless without their women, and Keith really pitied them.

'Anyway, huge changes, regardless,' Amy replied. 'Kenward goes. Suddenly the business map's redrawn, like Europe.'

'Kenward? That's a while now,' Keith said.

'But things haven't sorted themselves out,' Amy said. 'Big pickings, big grab-battles.'

'Bound to be, I expect,' Keith replied.

'Horton, Josh McCallion. I hear that was part of it,' Leyton said.

45

'God, was it?' Keith replied.

Amy drank and shook her head slowly. Naturally, she was grey under it all now, but kept herself a decent, rich blonde shade, not crazily bright.

'It would take clever cops to stitch up Claud Beyonton,' Leyton said.

'We've got clever cops,' Amy replied. 'You ever met Iles?'

'This was a grand victory for innocent men,' Keith said.

'A victory,' Amy replied. 'You're up against a threat, kid?'

'Suddenly, I don't feel complete without something, that's all,' Keith said. He left and thought about returning after five minutes to see if one of those suddenly friendly faces in there had gone over to Leyton and Amy's table to tell the latest about Keith Vine, a little failed chatterbox. Some customers might pick up more whispers than Leyton and Amy. But then, he decided, impossible. Leyton and Amy never missed anything. They had definitely liked him, especially her, as ever, and Keith had felt a true togetherness. This you would never get from Frogs.

Chapter 7

Harpur contacted Keith Vine and told him they must meet at once. 'Bring your girl,' Harpur said.

'Well, I—'

'Bring her,' Harpur replied. 'This is critical.' There was a duty to these two. It did not end because the trial did, or because Iles had a project.

'Where?' Keith asked.

Harpur could not go to Vine's place and he did not want him or both of them at Arthur Street again. Harpur used a string of quiet spots with his prime informant, Jack Lamb, but he would never reveal one of those to a nobody like Keith. 'Think of somewhere that suits the two of you,' he said.

'Becky wants to go to the antiques market in Elton Street.'

'Good.'

They met near what was called the Fun Clothes stall on the third floor, modes from the past. Becky was after a sixties' style loose gown for maternity, though she was hardly showing yet. 'You ought to get out,' he said. 'Go abroad now. We'll see to everything.'

'Why the rush?' Keith asked. He looked frightened but not enough. There was some stupid cockiness in this lad. 'What's changed, Mr Harpur?' he whispered. 'You weren't this way before.' He had his head back like a dog sniffing for quarry.

And Harpur saw he *was* sniffing for something. Well,

naturally. How these lads lived and saw the game. Vine would think Harpur had some cash interest in Kenward's former realm and wanted competition thinned. Keith probably regarded all police like that, but especially those around the top. What use being at the top, otherwise, and how had they got to the top if not like that? 'We don't think we can control Claud and the others post-trial,' Harpur said. 'The judge handed them a safe conduct.'

'You knew this before.'

'But my colleagues also say so, now.'

'Which colleagues?'

Keith was asking who else had a share. 'The Chief, Mr Iles. Wouldn't you like him to take you abroad for a while, Becky? Say, somewhere warm.'

She was fingering long, elegant old dresses on hangers, and he could tell she longed to say, *Yes, let's get out.* She was terrified. He also saw she had picked up Keith's suspicions. This girl had a mind, but not of her own. Many of them were like this. 'Well, it's for Keith to decide,' she said. 'Harpur, what sort of cop admits he can't control heavies? That the pit we're in, for God's sake?'

Yes, something like that. How could you tell beautifully pregnant Becky that an Assistant Chief wanted her lad made instant bait because detection was dead, Britain's criminal courts sick and ambush the last and only true weapon? Harpur had held back from putting protection/surveillance on Vine. Post-Erogenous, there was nobody good enough, and any people he chose would be too much at risk if Claud and his party suddenly turned up hunting. Another reason to get Vine and Becky off the patch. 'Has Keith explained what's on offer from us if you want setting up elsewhere?' Harpur replied. 'It's like Christmas.'

She shrugged and went behind a curtain to try on something she fancied.

Harpur said to Keith: 'There'd be a cash float as well as the house and moving expenses. Clothes wouldn't be a problem, I mean for you two and the baby. You could junk the combat jacket.'

She heard, and spoke in her weary, hard voice through the bit of pink curtain. 'Leave him alone, Harpur. I don't mind dressing second-hand, or the baby. Honestly I don't, Keith. I think of them as heritage clothes, wonderful, worthwhile things from the past.' She came out in the long blue and white dress looking beautiful. Often maternity could turn Harpur on. Christ, it would devastate him if Claud got to her and hers: such a duty to stop that. She was right to be terrified, but why didn't she *see* she was? She did, yet had to do loyalty to Vine. Iles wanted her for bait, too?

'What do you say, Keith?' she asked.

'About France?'

'No, this.'

'Oh, fine. Yes, lovely.'

'It's you,' Harpur said. 'You were thinking about France? Great idea.' While Becky looked at some other things, he drew Keith away to the men's clothes. It had been a mistake after all to make him bring that sharp, niggling partner. 'What's to keep you here, anyway, Keith?' Harpur asked. He knew the answer, but it was not one Vine could give.

There was a tail suit for eleven-fifty which looked big enough and appealed to Harpur. His father used to say every man should have a dark, formal outfit, including a hat, and Harpur sometimes felt the lack. The lapels showed a little wear, though the suit was definitely not more than forty years old.

'Where does Mr Iles come in all this?' Keith asked.

'All what?'

'He told you to get me abroad? This explains the change?' Becky rejoined them, still in the nice blue and white dress. The stall owner put the one she had been wearing into a carrier bag. She had heard. 'You think Iles told him to get you abroad, Keith?'

49

'Who else?' Keith replied.

She turned to face Harpur. 'You and Iles have some glowing commercial plans, post-Kenward Knapp?' she asked. 'That Iles needs a lot of cash – suits, shoes, smart wife, plus the extra he runs and pays for.'

Often women said things right out that the men would only think. Delicacy they despised. The women did not need to keep police sweet, or thought they didn't.

Harpur took the suit behind the curtain and put it on. With an ordinary collar and tie it was not at full power, but he thought he came over as a bit more than a head waiter. He rejoined them.

'It's you, Harpur,' Becky said.

'Will you wear it home, like Becky?' Keith asked.

'I think I will,' Harpur said. The stall lady put his suit into another carrier bag and then there was a long, loud bargaining while he got it reduced to nine, with a Homburg thrown in.

The three of them went down to the jewellery floor. Becky sauntered among the stalls. 'You owe it to Alby and McCallion, Keith,' Harpur said.

'How's that?'

'They wouldn't want the same to happen to you. They were wholesome lads in their greedy, blundering way.'

'Maybe I owe them something else – to put it right, what happened to them.'

'You tried. You can't do more. I mean that – you can't, not against this opposition.'

'Maybe I want to stay where I've lived all my life.'

'Die where you've lived all your life?'

'I can look after myself.'

'Oh?' Harpur asked.

'That doesn't mean weaponry.'

'Oh? Been over to The Hobart?'

'But look, I might think about France, anyway.'

'Think fast.'

Becky came back with some big, blue wooden beads

around her neck. Harpur thought they made her look somehow even more motherly and symbolic, the unhelpful cow. 'We're leaving now,' she said.

'Yes, I'll walk to the car with you,' Harpur replied.

'I refuse to be seen outside with you wearing that clobber and hat,' said Becky.

'That's reasonable,' Harpur replied. 'I think I'll stay and look for a silver cane.'

Chapter 8

Christ, Becky had to understand, had to. If Harpur and Iles wanted a piece of Kenward Knapp's late realm it must be golden, a land of silk and money. Well, everyone knew that already, including Becky, but when you had two prime figures like Harpur and Iles interested, and especially Iles, this meant something so juicy. Those two did not get out of bed for chicken-feed and the risks had to promise true rewards. Keith went over and over this with Becky, and she saw it, of course she saw it, she was not dim, but she kept on about France. This smart sod Harpur had reached her, scared her, that way he had – fooling about with the fucking commissionaire's suit to seem a clown and harmless, but getting the poison in all the time. This was how they ruled and built their deposit account. Why buy gear that probably Noah wore first to wow the beasts when Harpur knew he would soon have massive cash, if not already? This was a soften-up ploy, that's all.

Keith picked himself a workable post office, and would soon let Amy know a date for the Smith and Wesson 645. That was another visit to The Hobart, which bothered him a bit after what Harpur had said, but you could not order a gun by phone and pay the hire, even if you knew Leyton and Amy's number. So, there was this trip to say when he wanted it, then there'd be another to collect, and another after the job to take it back and buy the Makarov. These were hazards, but he would watch non-stop for any tail, and if he saw anything even half suspect he would skip the pub, go on somewhere else for the moment. Their best tail, Inspector Jeremy Jones, the one they called Erogenous, was dead, anyway.

Keith realized suddenly that he had stopped worrying about Claud and the others, and was only thinking of Harpur and his people as the enemy. This could be so crazy, and he knew he had to look out for those three as much as for police, and more, maybe. They had hate going for them as well as business. The thing about Becky was she really would be on his side if it was against someone else, such as Harpur, but as soon as they were by themselves she started giving all the points she had just pretended were stupid. And all the time pushing this kidmound at him like a writ, floodlighting his duties, saying without saying it he had to stop thinking about his ambitions and consider the unborn. Women like Becky could be clever yet not understand. They lacked outlook.

'Myself, I wonder if Harpur was trying to tell us something about the future,' Becky said.

'What's that mean?'

'Some police plan.'

'Their plan is to get a piece of Kenward or the lot. All police plans bigger than breathalyzing are about what's in it for them.'

'But if it's not, Keith? Harpur doesn't seem so bad. Is he warning us?'

'He's warning us off. They need a straight run. I don't jump just because he says so. You want that sort of man?'

'I want a man who's alive and—'

'Around to be the child's dad,' he recited.

'Is that so bad?'

They were in their rough kitchen washing up together, and he rested his suddy hand on her arm for quite a while, something really nice and domestic. She did deserve consideration. 'It's because I mean to be a true dad I need this business expansion, Becky love. Kids cost. Look, we don't want our child underprivileged. An income, year in year out, steady as a habit.'

The way Keith saw it, factors were drawing in on him, cornering him, but once he had the Makarov it would be fine and free, all choices open. Now, there was this pressure from Harpur and Becky and the thing about the Smith and Wesson was pressure, also. Once he told Amy he would take it for tomorrow or the day after, that was when the job had to be, and he hated being hemmed in like that, timetabled. Also, he hated them knowing he had the weapon for that one special day. They looked in the paper and saw some postmaster blown away by a .45 and they had a cosy little smile together. Those two were fine people, but they had a lot of knowledge, a lot of power.

With the Makarov it would be different. Ownership gave options. For instance, he could stay, he could go to France. Having the gun did not mean he would definitely stick around and look for some of Kenward. He could do some mulling over. This automatic was strength and liberty and peace of mind. There would be no hassle then about dates. And he could listen to all Becky's points and be really reasonable with them, feeling the gun in its holster against his chest, and ready if Claud turned up. Keith always reckoned himself very, very reasonable, even with some woman who tried the old sweet motherhood tricks.

If you were working this on your own, the kind of post office you wanted was small with only one behind the counter, and definitely not located inside a shop, as many were. A man or a woman running the post office, it did not matter which. The sight of a .45 very close affected most people the same, whatever sex. Women could sometimes be the most trouble, because they did not seem to realize what a big bullet from that range would do to your personality. Those post offices stuck at the back of a shop meant you would probably have quite a crew behind

54

while you were asking the postmaster or mistress for the cash. If there were two of you one could take care of all that, but on your own you did not want people you could not see. Some old lady might lead a charge swinging a cabbage.

Keith had found a pretty good one. It was a little dark hole of a place, though on a main road, with an oldish Pakistani running it, alone. You called him Postmaster but really he would only be a sub. Keith had been in for stamps; no cameras, but the grille protected by bullet-proof stuff. The Pakistani looked like he would be reasonable. Why should he want to die for Britain? Always the best way to get them in a useful spot was to be sending a parcel. That meant they had to come away from the grille and open the half-window at the end of the counter to take it in. This was when you muttered your few words and showed them the pistol. If necessary, you climbed over to convince them and check they bagged up all the money for you. You could reach in and grab, pull him or her against the gun muzzle and then ask where the panic button was. Once you located that you were all right, and you could make it clear what would happen if there was any move to it. Their voice would probably be gone in the fright, but they could point. You did not want to shoot, obviously.

Of course, if you picked a small PO for safety, you would not come out a millionaire. There would be at least hundreds, though, and probably thousands, as long as you chose a pension day and did it early before the grasping buggers had taken it all. Most likely they would be old notes, no tracing. The main object was to get enough for the Makarov, but something more would always help. There could be spare to give Becky and make her happy, or happier.

He did a nice parcel and addressed it in plain, anonymous block capitals to a lady called Mrs Myfanwy Williams at 10, Lloyd George Street, Swansea. A big

Welsh town like Swansea would be sure to have a Lloyd George Street, so if there was a Mrs Myfanwy Williams there she might soon be getting a great present of an empty cereal box and a worn-out teddy bear, which he had lifted from someone's refuse sack in the street.

Chapter 9

He took his time at the door of the post office, glancing about for a while, getting a picture of the road and the shops and offices near by. But Christ, was any place more cosy for a hold-up? They could have put a sign outside, *Rob Me*. The office stood half screened by a hedge, no window on to the road for witnesses, and a good solid door that could be locked from inside for the raid. Could be, had been. Harpur loitered a little longer in the street, as if doing the geography. He knew what he would find inside, and it would wait.

Apparently, an elderly man had wanted to get in shortly after 9 a.m. and couldn't. Assuming there was some delay in opening, he strolled on to the newspaper shop. When he returned in ten minutes the door was unlocked and he went in and found the place as if empty, but not. Mr Ali was on the floor, hidden by the counter. The old man saw him when he reached the grille, flapping his pension book. Mr Ali was face down and at first the old man thought a heart attack or stroke. He spoke, asked Mr Ali what was wrong, but had no answer. Then he saw the blood edging out from under the sub-postmaster's cardigan on the linoleum and did not know what to think, except that he would have to do without his pension for a while. He noticed the safe door was open. There were papers in there, but he saw no money.

The old man retreated and walked in his slow style to the nearest shop where he reported the situation, though without mentioning blood. His eyes were not too great, and he wondered now if he had seen right. Two men from the shop returned with him and one climbed over the half-door at the parcels end and crouched alongside Mr Ali, calling his name, asking what had happened. When he took Mr Ali by one shoulder and lifted him a little he knew what had happened and used the phone back there to call for help.

Now, Harpur felt he had surveyed the locality well enough and must stop stalling. He went in. Garland said: 'Pass-the-parcel job, sir. He's been hit by something very large, probably an S and W .45. Two shots, both chest. The parcel's not much use to us, of course. Somehow, he forgot to write the sender's name and address on it, and the destination doesn't exist.'

'I had Wayne Timberlake's note on what the old man said. He saw nothing, heard nothing? Two shots from a thing so big. That's noisy.'

'Possibly silenced. Anyway, he might have been on his way to the newspaper shop by then. There's traffic din at that hour. We're asking in the shops and offices. Our lad could pop a mask on with the cover of that hedge and pocket it again before he left. Then he's just someone else on his way to work.'

Harpur disliked post office jobs. They always seemed to him drab, the likely takings minor for the risk and possible damage. They fell below Harpur's idea of himself, but his idea of himself must be wrong, because post offices did get robbed, and always he had to attend the after-maths. There was something else. Not long ago he had killed a post office raider called Webb in one of those ambushes which Iles considered the necessary future of policing. Harpur had shot Webb to stop Webb shooting Erogenous Jones. It had been utterly justifiable, and the inquiry said so. All the same, Harpur's uneasiness with post office crimes had grown and stuck. Soon afterwards, Erogenous was killed by somebody else, anyway.

'Who the hell wields a .45?' Garland asked.

'There's all sorts about these days.'

'The Post Office people say between two thousand one hundred and three thousand two hundred gone. It looks as if Mr Ali came to the parcel aperture but then resisted, possibly tried for the button.'

'How do people get so brave? Why?'

'Folk in public service are often like this, Colin.'

'That right? Are we?'

'Post offices always turn you mystical, sir.'

Chapter 10

Keith said: 'Yes, of course I like the one you bought at the antiques place, it's lovely. Real style and it would take someone with real style to spot it, love. All I said is, get yourself another, something new, that's all, so you can look great in two fashions – that grand, old one, and a modern-day model, change and change about. Why not?'

'I buy there because it's cheap.'

'I know it, Becky, and it's thoughtful. Many a pregnant girl wouldn't bother, I do know it. But, look, there's a bit of cash now. What I say is, use it. And where's better to use it than on mother and babe?' He kissed her forehead.

'They're pricey, up-to-date maternity things.'

'Yes.' But he did not bring out some great fat wad of notes like a bookie, knowing that would be stupid, a proclamation. First he felt in one pocket and produced four twenties and a ten, and then he scoured around the rest of his trousers and jacket like a gull on a tip and eventually piled up three hundred on the kitchen table. 'See how far this goes,' he said.

She looked at it and left it there.

'This comes from a pile I've been owed for months,' he said. 'My share from a good piece of business. It was in assets till now, not cash, that's all.'

'This means we're staying?' she asked, gazing at him in that clever-clever, stare-stare, sad-sad way she used sometimes.

'Why, darling? Why should it have to mean that, some decent funds from way back?'

'It's a feeling I've got, Keith.' She had the suffering voice on, too. He could handle that.

'Me, I've made no choices yet,' he replied. 'I'm looking at all possibilities, Becky. My feeling now is I can do – *we* can do just what we like. No pressure.'

'Why?'

'What?'

'Why do you feel like that now? The money?'

'The money – and more. I've got this sense of, oh, I don't know, it sounds fruity, but this sense of poise. Yes, poise. It comes from you, Becky. It's only and totally from you and the child. This feeling fatherhood's approaching, it takes hold of a man, gives him vision. Poise.'

'You were never short of it.'

'But now, really solid, established. We're entitled.' He gave a bit of a shout. 'That's it! Suddenly I feel sure we're entitled.'

She leaned forward and returned the kiss, on his forehead, but it was like an auntie's kiss. *There, there, little lad, go and play some more.* They were seated at the kitchen table drinking tea, Becky in the blue and white robe. Keith thought she looked like one of the three wise men. Maybe it was not just the robe, but because she wanted to travel towards some spot where everything would start new again. And she *could* be wise. If you picked a girl who could think as well as screw, you had to put up with that now and then. He gathered the money, pulled one of her hands across the table towards him, placed the notes in it and folded her fingers around them. Things could start new again here, too. 'I'm being forced,' she said, but did not release the notes.

'Right. If Claud was going to try anything they'd have tried by now. That's something they'd do when they were hot. It wears off.'

'Claud's face is not for doing things when he's hot. I

61

shouldn't think he's ever hot. Just bloody evil, and unforgetful. *It wears off.* That's what I mean – it sounds as if you're going to stay. You feel really safe all of a sudden. Why?'

'No decisions at all yet,' he replied. 'As a matter of fact, I'm going to drift up to Ralphy Ember's club tonight, see if I can bump into Stan Stanfield for a chat about France.'

'Honestly, Keith?'

'Of course.'

'Oh, I would, would love to get out,' she cried. 'A good night's sleep somewhere, not this listening for doors, windows, listening for someone cursing a grass. Do you know, Keith, in Provence, France, there's actually a place called Grasse which I hear is very nice? You see, *everything* would be different there.'

'Stan's a lad with very positive ideas,' Keith replied.

Never expect to see Stanfield in a place like The Hobart. This pub and the whole Cork Street area he would regard as fish-and-chippy. He had worked in France, and considered himself sophisticated, even with that stupid, huge sodding moustache. Plus, Stanfield was supposed to be descended from some genuine artist last century who was good at boats. Stan would definitely like the bit of polish the Monty tried to give, regardless of Ralphy Ember's panics and sweats and the tarts and layabouts.

You had to kowtow to Stanley. You had to speak to him like to the admiral of the fleet or an artistic offspring. He was there tonight, talking to Ralph across the bar when Keith arrived, the moustache wagging like a tattered old sheep's arse. They both gave him a smile that looked friendly enough. He had to feel his way here, like at The Hobart. Nobody stopped playing pool when he came in, there was no sudden, hard silence. It could be all right. If the word had not reached The Hobart, probably it would not reach here. Claud was a member, but perhaps he was keeping things quiet. Or perhaps he still did not know which mouth gave them to Harpur. Yes, bloody perhaps. Anyway, he could answer Claud with a decent surprise now, times eight.

Ralphy was called away to deal with something and Keith went and stood alongside Stanfield. 'Stan,' he said, 'I've been thinking about France. I'd be glad of some insights.'

'Why? You've got to get out? Harpur near on something?'

'Just looking for expansion, freshness, that's all. I'm becoming a family, June, and it makes you wonder.'

'France? You'd fit in well there, Keith. You've got the poise.'

'Poise? That's going it a bit. Just I need something new.'

'What the French say – *avoir besoin d'un changement*.'

'Sounds about right.'

Keith ordered Kressmann Armagnacs for the two of them. He paid with a ten and took a long time finding it again, like with Becky. You did not trumpet. 'Or I might stay, Stan.'

'It's a toss-up.'

'Stan, people wonder – why did you come back? It's better here?'

'Avoir besoin d'un changement.'

'The point is, it *could* be better here.'

'Well, it could be,' Stanfield said.

'I mean, especially now.'

'It could be,' Stanfield replied.

'But it's not something for a man on his own.'

Stanfield stood. He was big and blond. Women went for him, the loud sod. 'Let's take a table, Keith.' He called to Ralphy: 'Keith's thinking of France. I'm going to give him a guided tour.' He found a place under a framed, group photograph of a Monty trip to Florence or Las Vegas, somewhere like that. Ralphy and his wife were in it, Ralphy giving a half-profile, so you could see the Chuck Heston likeness.

'I know you prefer working with your own team, Stan. Beau Derek, and so on.'

'I'm always looking around,' he replied.

'I'm feeling pretty confident, but I need someone with experience. Well, I suppose I mean your leadership.'

Stanfield moved his hand under the table like about to give Keith a quick feel, but instead touched the outside of his jacket pocket, where the automatic was. 'You're thinking of serious business then,' he said. 'Been over to Leyton?'

'It would be, well, a real crime to let this chance go.'

'Kenward's? You could get crushed in the queue. Look what happened to Alby and Josh McCallion. Is the weapon hire or purchase?'

'Purchase. That's what I'm trying to say, Stan. I'm thinking long term. Those two, Alby and Josh, they were treasures, but so minor. I don't have to tell you. They had no planning, no vision.'

'You knew them?'

'It's what I heard, Stan.'

'Purchase?' Stanfield replied. 'You're into good money?'

'It's what I mean, Stan. Lately I find I've got quite a decent business approach.'

'That gun been fired?' Stanfield asked.

'New.'

'Only, some postie got blasted yesterday morning and around three grand gone.'

'I read it,' Keith replied.

'But that would be a hire weapon, I should think,' Stanfield said.

'That how they do it? This is what I'm saying about your experience, leadership. You know how things work.'

'Some poor sod hires it next week and gets caught, he's down for the postmaster, and whatever else.'

'Why I'd always buy,' Keith replied.

'And something in this for Beau?'

'Well, Beau's safes, isn't he? I mean, this is not that kind of trade, Stan. This is money by hand week after week on the street. That's the beauty of it. Habit cash.'

'Beau's adaptable.'

'I don't say no, but—'

'I shouldn't think I could do much without Beau,' Stanfield replied. 'We've shared a lot of stresses. We know each other's work patterns, you see, Keith.'

Probably he was banging Beau's woman and had to make sure they earned enough to stay. 'If you think he could be useful, Stan, am I the one to argue? Like I said, your leadership.'

'I'm going to think about this, Keith. That purchase – it's impressive, shows solidity.'

'Christ, Stan, I knew if I was going to talk to Stan Stanfield I had to come with a real case, real prospects.'

'Keep Ralphy out of it,' Stanfield replied.

'Well, naturally.'

'He'll be sniffing, seeing us in private chat. Ralphy's a great taker. Why he's so fucking rich on no risk.'

'More Armagnac, Stan?' Keith replied.

'My turn.'

'No, let me. Celebration.'

'Sudden funds?'

'No, I mean celebrate this "private chat".'

'I said I'm going to think about it, that's all.'

'Good enough for me, when it's Stanley Stanfield doing the thinking.'

Chapter 11

People with something deep and intimate to discuss in the Monty often went to that secluded table used by Vine and Stan Stanfield, and years ago Ralph Ember had decided he would be slack not to bug it. He hid a microphone behind the club trip picture which hung near. This never produced much understandaþle business material, though, because of background hullabaloo from the customers and jukeboxes, and after a few months Ember had removed it. He felt easier when it was gone. A mike behind a photograph was so standard, and he had always been terrified when a really dangerous crew went to sit there, because boys like that expected spies. Ember used to watch and sweat in case one of them did a check. All sorts fussed about privacy.

But tonight he did not really need a bug. When a lad of Stan Stanfield's scale drifted off for a private session with some brassy infant he hardly knew, you could guess something was on the move. And probably the only item grand enough to interest Stanley these days was the late Knapp's realm, which fascinated Ralph, too. Stanley Stanfield loved to think he had status, and perhaps he did have a bit. He'd fucked up somehow in France, or he would not be back, but he managed to keep the details quiet and so he could still act unbeatable.

The kid with him, Vine? This was a kid with a gun in his jacket pocket, probably an automatic. You could follow that nice square, homely shape through the material. Possibly he had had a gun in his pocket before, but not often, and he hadn't learned yet how to stroll as if he didn't. Nonchalance was a closed book. He went in for that crazy, ready-aye-ready walk, crouched a bit forward in a challenge, wearing a bloody naff combat jacket. His hand kept touching the weapon outline, like someone doing worry beads. This was the sort of kid who could have killed the postie for three piffling grand, and the smile and cockiness looked like pay-day. To Keith Vine, that might be real money, enough for him to treat his girl and step up from hiring fire-power to buying. Not even someone as bouncy mad as this kid would hold on to the .45 that did the postie. In any case, the thing in his pocket was not big enough. A .45 would be a good eight and a half inches. His piece was more like six.

While Stan and Keith were at their table, Ember sauntered over a couple of times, gathering glasses, sprucing ashtrays, but they were too fly. He heard nothing except Vine speak the words 'your leadership' to Stanley, in the sort of hushed, unquestioning way Eva might have said it to Adolf. You could tell Vine had picked up a stack of spending cash recently by the way he pretended not to have much, all that slow, showy mystery tour of his pockets. In any case, he would not have the cheek to chat up Stan Stanfield unless he'd done something eminent lately, such as wipe out a sub-postmaster among stamps. Armagnac Keith Vine did not really need, he had adrenalin. So, he asks Stan about France, thinking of going there to live. Thinking of going there to live, bollocks. This boy was after an enterprise, and on his doorstep, not abroad. Ember felt a bit pissed off by him, edging into the main game, lumbering the scene. There were enough at that already.

He felt a bit sad for him, also. He heard Vine's girl, Becky, had a babe aboard. Ember had always regarded children as a totally serious, worthwhile thing, and Becky was a sweet-looking, graceful, very bright girl he often considered screwing himself. Didn't this stupid kid, Keith, see the sort of hazard he was giving the fine mother and this child-to-be? But at Vine's age, that was a real rousing, dazing mixture – the money, the gun, and proud memories of din and finality at the post office.

Ember said goodbye and drove across town to see Claud Beyonton, leaving the bar staff and his wife to run the club for a few hours. Normally, he went home mid-evening. He was doing a full-time university degree course up the road, and liked a few hours for study and writing. Then he would go back to the Monty later and stay until closing, around 2 a.m. But tonight he would skip academic work. It was important to talk to Claud. Sight of Stanfield and Vine together sharpened the urgency. Huge share-outs would be around soon. Although most thought Ember rich, there were always money worries, mostly from his love life, of course. Now and then he wished to God he did not look like Heston. He longed to talk to Chuck and ask him if he had this continual fawning from women, and how he dealt with it.

All sorts of teams wanted sole control of Kenward's former glittering outfit. Since his death, it ran piecemeal, full of small-timers. Even nothings like Alby Horton and McCallion tried for a corner. That shambles could not continue. Some suitable combination was sure to take the lot. Ember would back Claud. Tonight, in the club, he had thought for a second or two about Stanfield and Keith Vine, and wondered if he should make an approach there, seek an alliance. But Vine was another nothing, and Stanfield's c.v. lacked all mention of drugs trading. Although he and Beau Derek did very calibre robberies, that was a different diploma altogether.

Ember preferred the look of Claud and partners. They had that fireproof gloss since the acquittals, and there was also a sound history in pushing. It was not up to Knapp's, nowhere near, nobody's was, but they had the beginnings, and showed business flair by getting rid of Alby and Josh

McCallion. This was the other point against Vine. He had worked with those boys, at least off and on, and maybe more. He could be on Claud's list, and the automatic in Vine's pocket would not help him much if so. Plus, there had to be a bit of a stench around Keith Vine. It would make sense for a confed. of Alby and Josh to try to get those who did them jailed. Was Vine the still, small secret voice that talked to Harpur? That would make him very breakable.

Chapter 12

Harpur had a call from Jack Lamb. 'Know a Johnny called Keith, Colin?'

'Surname or first name?'

'Speculate.'

'What about him?'

'Not on an open line.'

This phrase ran Lamb's life. When made a lord, he should put it on his escutcheon in Latin. Probably he would not be, though, not even if Wilson got back into Downing Street.

'Haven't heard from you for a while, Jack.'

'I've been freezing you.'

'I thought so.'

'You hurt me, Col.'

'How did I manage that?'

'Not on an open line. I hope you're not devoted to this kid, Col.'

'Which kid?'

'The one mentioned.'

'What's happened?'

'Or to happen.'

'When?'

Lamb did not answer but suggested a meeting at the old anti-aircraft gun emplacement they sometimes used as a rendezvous, on a hill just outside the city. Jack liked military settings, and would often dress to match. If it was costume time, Harpur decided he could give the morning suit and Homburg a run. He was tired of looking subfusc against Lamb in his gear. Harpur's daughters knew nothing of the outfit, and when he came downstairs wearing it they gazed long at him, silently at first. He had failed to find a cane to go with the ensemble.

He said: 'I thought the suit must be thirty or forty years old, but inside the breast pocket there's a name and date from 1911. Fantastic.'

'Was that a good year for suits?' Hazel asked.

Jill said: 'I've definitely seen you looking more stupid, Dad. It's clever to try other styles. There's got to be something, somewhere to make you seem all right. Stick at it.'

At the gun-site, Lamb did not comment on the clothes for a while, either. 'Well, I get many signals about this lad, Col. He's so sure he has a future, the idiot.'

'A lot like that these days. Is he young? It's the buoyantly questing Thatcher generation coming through, probably.'

'In and out of The Hobart,' Lamb replied. 'Here's the procedure, Col: turns up and talks; turns up again and talks; turns up again and doesn't talk much but takes something; turns up again, doesn't talk at all, brings something, takes something. How do you read that, Col? Leyton Harbinger and Amy central each time, obviously.'

'Is it Keith's local?' Harpur replied. 'I mean, the regularity. Working-class spot? A racing-pigeon club there? Did it look like pigeons they were swapping? Any cooing?'

'Ah, pigeons.' Jack Lamb was perhaps the greatest informant ever. Oh, forget fucking *perhaps*, he was. People like Keith Vine were only starters and would never match him, even if they lived to twenty-eight. Lane and Iles could know about Keith, but never about Lamb. As Jack said, there had been a bad shut-down lately between him and Harpur, and Harpur found it like working blindfold in a pit. Yes, Jack was supreme, a brilliant font, and you tried to tell him nothing. Probably he would know it, anyway. You listened. You listened and you'd better believe it. This was how a detective's mucky liaison with his grass operated. It is more blessed to receive than to give. That would be Harpur's escutcheon motto. As to title, Lord Harpur of Grey Areas.

Lamb said: 'The two-way traffic of that fourth visit fascinates, don't you think? Something pleasant yet private from Keith to Leyton and Amy and something pleasant yet private from Leyton and Amy to Keith. I mean, something from Keith to Leyton and Amy as well as money.'

'This sounds like a business deal.'

'Piss off, Col. You know this boy, you know what's happening. I think you look stately. Anyone else, that ensemble would bring real refinement to, take them into the Neville Chamberlain class. Clearly, it can't do that for you, but the hat makes you seem reliable, even honourable, glimpsed in this half-light.'

'Thanks, Jack.'

Lamb himself wore a khaki, cavalry bum-freezer coat, green riding breeches, brown gauntlet gloves, calf-high boots and a Montgomery-style black beret with large silver badge. He carried a leather-clad cane. Harpur had seen most of this turnout before. Jack was losing zing. Harpur felt he had scored.

'Do I interpret the Hobart pattern or do you?' Lamb asked. He did not wait for a reply, though. 'Keith goes first to make sure he's all right with Leyton and Amy, no serious doubts about him. Brave boy, let's admit it.'

'What's that mean, Jack – "all right"? Why shouldn't this Keith be "all right"?'

Fondly, Lamb ran his gloved hand along the concrete perimeter of the gun-site and gazed down past a string of pylons at the city's dubious glow. 'Troops up here in the 1940s had all that lovely human hive in their care,' he said. 'Now, it's you and me. I believe we can do it, Col.

A great detective, his aide.' Lamb stiffened and saluted, fingers up touching the badge, the way Monty did it on old, hit-em-for-six newsreels.

'Iles says the detective is dead.'

'Has he seen you in those clothes and hat? He'd never speak like that if so. Blasphemy.'

'Thanks, Jack. But he means the whole species, not just me.'

'Many see Iles as a saint,' Lamb replied.

'Not *many*, Jack. *Several*, and that includes himself.'

'Includes you? But then, you used to have his wife. Would anyone do that to a saint, even you, Col? When I say "all right", Keith has to make sure, hasn't he, that he's *persona grata* at The Hobart, and especially with Leyton and Amy?'

'This lad's done something to offend them?' Harpur replied.

'That was hurtful, too, Col – going to a babe like Keith Vine as tipster.'

'The Hobart? This is a big pub on a corner, with a parrot?' Harpur replied.

'Well, he's all right with Leyton and Amy, regardless. He's a pretty kid. Amy's old juices rumble. These days and nights Leyton gets his kicks sniffing cordite, and she's pent up. So, they agree a menu and price and on visit two Keith arrives to say when he'll want to partake. And then visit three. This could be important for you, Col – the date. As we've seen, something passes on visit three, from Leyton and Amy to Keith. Something passes from Keith to them, too, but only payment. Probably an instalment.'

'You're at The Hobart yourself to watch all this, Jack?'

'Zombie,' Lamb replied. 'I keep an expensive pair of eyes there.'

'Someone I know?'

'If you've got anything that baffles you happening soon after visit three – Well, that's what I mean about the date, Col. For instance, a crime. You deal with crimes, don't you? And even you are sometimes baffled. Not dead, baffled.'

'What date?' Harpur replied.

'Last Sunday at The Hobart. If, say, you had something on the Monday or Tuesday. I don't know. Either a pension day, for example? Wednesday, blow me, he's at The Hobart again, looking seasoned. That's the word I get from my hired eyes, Col: oh, yes, a vocab. there as well as perceptiveness, all for the one charge. And then this complicated interchange, Amy still overheating at sight of Keith and seeking urgent frottage from her chair, but he's off into all his tomorrows with a happy whistle. Gratefully returning something and taking something else, perhaps as a permanency?'

Sometimes up here, Jack would make explosive noises with his lips and point a hand high, like an ack-ack battery taking on the *Luftwaffe*. Tonight, though, he seemed in dreamier mood. '*Kiss me goodnight, Sergeant Major,*' he remarked. 'That would be one of the numbers they sang to themselves as they knocked the Heinkels down. *Tuck me in my little wooden bed.*'

'This Keith is a busy lad,' Harpur said.

'I told you, he expects a future. In a way it's forgivable. You stood by him in the witness box, Col, and gave him heart. I've trained you well.' He did another bit of a war song. 'Iles is never going to let those three escape, is he – Claud and so on? But is he, Col? Iles will use this kid's confidence, turn him into bait, so Claud etcetera can be gunned by police marksmen in the standard self-defence? What I mean when I say a saint.'

They walked side by side around the parapet of the big gun pit, Lamb still humming the song, rapping his breeches with the cane. 'Warrior ghosts, Col,' he whispered. 'I see them, hear them in their boots, smell their Park Drive ciggies. Would one could have been there too, preserving Britain from the plague. But I say again the same duty falls now. We're needed. We're ready.'

74

Harpur said: 'This has been a worthwhile trip, regardless, Jack. I wouldn't want you to think you're wasting my time.'

'Conscripts, yes, Col, yet their souls soared with those shells, too, magnificently ripping into fuselages and people. Then, a couple of days later Keith's in the Monty at the plot table, tooled up, and he's with—' He stopped, heavy with loathing, and faced Harpur, staring down at him. Harpur was hefty, but Lamb towered like another wide pylon. 'Well, guess, Col. You tell me who he was with.'

Harpur thought he could guess, but did not. 'Are we still talking about this lad Keith?'

'Who was he with, Col?'

'What, you mean with Panicking Ralph Ember himself?'

'Ralphy's looking elsewhere for partnership.'

It had to be Stanley Stanfield. That would explain so much. Harpur said: 'The Monty is a wonderful focus for this city, like another cathedral, or Buckingham Palace.'

'Stanfield,' Lamb replied.

'Stanfield. Hang on. Yes, I recall this one. Stanley, yes? Is he still about, then?'

'You know he is, you double-dealing sod.'

'Discussing what with Stanfield?' Harpur replied.

'Those tomorrows.'

'You've got expensive eyes at the Monty, too, Jack? And ears?'

'That table, you know it, nobody can get close enough to hear, and Ralphy's taken the mike away, so nil chance of eavesdropping a tape, either,' Lamb replied.

'This boy Keith seems to—'

'I agree with you, Stanfield is horseshit, yes, that high-born strut, the slimy moustache, but quality horseshit. A kid like that able to drift in and tête-à-tête with him – this has to embrace prospects, Col. It's the birth of a confederacy.'

Harpur said: 'Is Stanfield still trying to—?'

'I've no words from this meeting whatsoever,' Lamb replied. 'But it was intense and continuously amicable, fortified by Kressmann Armagnac, Keith Vine paying. This was the report one had from there – "intense and continuously amicable, fortified by Kressmann Armagnac, Keith Vine paying".'

They walked back towards their cars, parked separately off the road and hidden by woodland. Harpur saw now why Lamb had suddenly resumed contact. Jack hated, feared, Stanley Stanfield. It was a steamy matter of Jack's young, lovely, live-in girlfriend, Helen Surtees, ex latter-day punk and a town hall ballet-class pal of Denise's. Stanfield had been very taken with Helen, perhaps still was. By now, there might be much more to it. Stanfield was nearly a couple of decades younger than Jack and glamorous, despite the moustache. Jack must worry whether he could hold on to a girl like Helen, still not twenty, Lamb being up there, touching fifty, full of money and kudos and possessions and property, yes, but still touching fifty, too many gold teeth. Harpur could understand these anxieties over a young girlfriend, though he himself would only be a few years older than Stanfield.

Lamb's tactics now were what you would expect from a grass of his prim grandeur. He did not pass on everything about all the villains he knew. That would be foul and dishonourable. Finkdom. He needed motivation, not just quid pro quo from Harpur, and hate and fear and jealousy were the best prompts ever. 'Did you tell me once Stanfield had actually tried something with Helen, Jack? Got really close?'

Lamb ignored this. But in his first rage a while ago Jack had mentioned something of the sort: maybe it had even been forcible, maybe charm only. Of course, it was possible Helen liked Stanfield, too. Lamb could never concede that, though. Stanfield did pull women. Harpur thought Stan excited even Denise. Once before Jack had tried to get Stanfield celled and long-term removed by pointing Harpur towards him and his burglaries. It hadn't worked. Stanfield stayed free, and Lamb stayed bitter and distant, until now.

'Naturally, there's a buzz around that you and Iles are looking for a quota of the Kenward Knapp inheritance yourselves,' Lamb said. 'Frustrated by policing – death of the detective, as you mentioned. Iles living very rich, earning very mediocre.'

'How's Helen?' Harpur replied.

'Col, I don't deserve such adoration, such unmitigated passion.'

'It's the love of women, Jack – constant, uncompromising, elevated.'

'Right.'

A tragedy for Keith Vine that he should be dragged into the ambit of Lamb's desperate jealousy because of a little chat with Stanfield.

Chapter 13

Curled on the back seat of his car, Keith watched Claud Beyonton's house through the rear window. It was a suitable, very quiet street of dim semis. This was a street where Keith knew he could do well, again. Why the hell should he stay home with the shivers, biting his nails, nursing the Makarov, waiting as scared as Becky for Claud and his couple of hounds to pounce? Any pouncing, Keith could do. This did not mean he was into blood-lust, anything like that. But a man with a real future turned situations around, put himself in control. He did not cower, never played victim. Initiative. This was what maturity meant, such as the Falklands Task Force. Could he risk Beyonton getting into the nest near Becky and the child-to-be, for God's sake? Keith would pick locations. And Keith would start and finish whatever was to happen.

You never did a watch job head-on to the target, because of the obviousness, the hard, staring eyes and unmoving head behind a windscreen, as seen in TV cop dramas. Of course, doing things Keith's way was one of the oldest ploys known to real businessmen and real police, so it might not fool Claud, but you stuck to what you had been taught. In any case, Keith was a good distance from the house, a few parked vehicles shielding him without blocking the view.

He had bought twine and a sail-repair needle and stitched himself a rough shoulder holster from the canvas of Becky's old rucksack. Then he had made a harness with a couple of leather belts. He loved handicraft skills and it would have been stupid to buy a holster, because police always talked to gun shops after a shooting, and might talk some more, if things developed today. He enjoyed the hard grip of the leather around his back and chest and the sweet solidity of a paid-for gun against his armpit. These felt like maturity, too, and he thanked God it had come early to him like many of those great composers. Sometimes he thought Becky did not realize how lucky she was to find someone so all-round, though he did not hold this against her. She could only know part, because stress was bad for the pregnancy. She would carry that weight, he would take all the other.

Claud was inside the house, he knew it. His Saab stood on the drive and about an hour ago Harry Foster had arrived in a Sierra and gone in. He was wearing some rich, flapping, bright brown overcoat with the collar up, for raciness, not cold. Keith could have knocked him over with the Makarov – just a little spring along the pavement for a perfect, close, two-handed, unwitnessed focus on the chest and then two shots, one for luck, again as the textbooks said, and which he now knew did work very neatly. Also it could be seen as one shot each for Alby Horton and McCallion. It did not matter about witnesses, anyway. Nobody talked these days. People had learned the new rules. Harry was probably not even armed. Since that trial they thought they would live for ever. Harry did not hurry into Claud's place or look about for a possible ambush. He sauntered, flashing the overcoat, a ginger-plumed sitting duck.

But Harry was only Harry. He would not do. Whereas to see off Claud would be to see off all threat. There would be no need then to think for even two seconds about Becky's worries and France, as if he ever did. Those others could not keep going as a syndicate without Claud. They needed the leadership, mutts. They would come apart. This meant not just dropping any hunt for Keith, they would have no chance of the late Kenward's wondrous bits and pieces. That was Keith's double objective. Oh, yes, Harry would have looked beautiful as a corpse in the gutter and he had earned it on Alby and Josh, but all the major problems would remain, only worse, because Claud was bound to know who had done it and who might be next if he delayed. When mature, you had to think things through, not settle for quick joys such as Harry shot. Keith was going to be a father and must create a long, worthwhile future. When he considered that future, Becky and the child were definitely parts of it and near the centre, regardless. They were entitled. She had bought a new green and gold maternity dress with some of the money and looked serene and motherly in that one, too, and much richer.

He practised three or four times pulling the gun from its holster, not to be Wyatt Earp, just for ease and familiarity. He did not take his eyes off the front door of Claud's semi. Keith knew he had a gift for this sort of work. And others would soon recognize it. Perhaps they did already. At Ember's club the other night, when Stan Stanfield leaned across and touched the gun, it might seem so sharp, but probably all it meant was Keith Vine now looked the experienced kind who would carry a decent piece as routine. That action by Stan was a warm gesture between equals, like great Jap sumo fighters bowing first. Keith was coming on to the big scene. No, sod it, suddenly he was right there. Hadn't he proved at the post office that he could manage a good outing, and he had responsibilities to a new generation. Keith's bouncy soul told him he was a different being from the one who tapped at Harpur's window in the night, so nervy and frail – so pathetic. Harpur he had outgrown. Stanfield had pretended to be unsure and sniffy about an alliance, because that's how Stanfield was, the big-headed, Euro dick. All the same, Stanfield realized he was talking to someone major though young, no question. Stanfield would soon come wagging that sad moustache, and wagging money, begging for partnership.

But then, when Claud's door suddenly opened and he came out in one of his damn executive suits and a super-gleam white shirt, Keith's certainties fell apart. Claud was not alone. Of course, Keith had half expected Harry as well, and thought he could cater for that. There were four of them, though. Keith had been just about to leave his car for the approach, hand under his jacket on the pistol, but stopped now, edged down into the corner of the seat, still watching, taking real care. There would have to be a postponement, that was certain. It would be mad, boyish, to try to take on four, even with a top-class automatic. Gerry Reid was with them, which also could have been half expected. But what really shook Keith was to see Panicking Ralph Ember there, and there like he belonged – easy with them, even a partner. It stole Keith's strength for a few seconds. He had heard a million whispers about new teams to take over from Kenward, but none of them put Claud and Ralphy together. God, wasn't Ember much too big, way beyond meetings in a semi? Ember had worked with some of the greatest, let down really prize people.

You thought you had a situation clear in your head, and then something like this. Suddenly he was almost a kid again, dazed at finding what the big boys were doing on the quiet. If Ralphy was working with Claud Beyonton and the others it would make a mighty combine. Who else would get a look in? Oh, sure, Ember could fall into sweats and panics, but he had substance, power, durability. Just look at his house, Low Pastures, and the spread. The story was he might have got the property from another operator, Caring Oliver, missing now, maybe dead, and maybe missing now maybe dead because of a ploy pulled by Ember himself. Just look at the way he piled it up and stayed out of jail. Ralphy had a golden-road career.

You could see immediately how different he was from

these three now, outside the house. Ember did not dawdle or dream or parade his clothes. He moved fast, eyes everywhere. This was someone looking for hazard and for openings and able to deal with both. Keith went lower in his car. They all climbed into the Saab, and Claud drove away. Keith stayed in the back of the vehicle for a few minutes, trying to sort out what it all signified. He did not follow. He was too slow getting around to his driving seat and anyway, with Ember in the Saab, there was no chance of tailing unspotted. Keith dredged for his morale. There had been a moment as Ember gazed about in that bloody all-conquering El Cid style of his when Keith found himself thinking again of France. Becky could be right. Grass to Grasse was better than dust to dust. He was so lucky to have a bright girl like that to look after him while holding back on certain questions. Priceless. She had to be entitled to a point of view.

Chapter 14

Jill opened the door while Harpur still had his key in the lock. 'There's a lady here to see you, Dad,' she said. Very pretty. Rebecca. She's in a real fret, but Hazel and I have been soothing her and saying how nice you are although police.'

'She knows already.'

In the big living room, Becky was seated with Hazel on the settee, drinking Ovaltine. Becky wore a smart new maternity dress in green and gold. There must be money about. Yes, she was very pretty, but perhaps she had not been sleeping much.

'Becky has a message,' Hazel said. Harpur's daughters were good at welcoming people, giving them comfort, making them talk, promising anyone with troubles prompt miracles from Daddy.

'Well, perhaps you children could go into the kitchen now,' Harpur replied.

'We know the message,' Jill said. 'It's all right.'

'She wants to leave, that's all,' Hazel said. 'She wants to get out of this area, at once.'

'I've heard about this,' Harpur replied.

'On her own,' Hazel said.

'Yes,' Becky said.

'Things have changed, you see, Dad,' Jill told him.

Yes, they had, if Jack Lamb was reading right. Usually, Jack *did* read right, even when off balance through love and hate. 'Which things?' he asked.

'To do with the man she lives with,' Hazel replied.

'How changed?'

'And she needs your urgent help, that's all, Dad,' Jill told him.

'We said we knew you'd do all within your power,' Hazel told him.

'Of course,' Harpur replied.

Jill clapped her hands and grinned. 'There's going to be a baby, you know.'

'That so?' Harpur replied.

Hazel stared at Becky. 'Look – God – it's not—'

'What?' Becky asked.

'Not *his*?'

'Of course it's not, Hazel,' Jill shrieked.

'No, no, I knew really, but, well, Dad gets around,' Hazel said. 'And you're so pretty and young, Becky, and coming here like this. My dad's lovely, but he's very ... well, very loving. You know, he meets a lot of people. Women. But if it was his he would stand by you, if you wanted him to. You wouldn't need to run. Though he looks rough he's all right, really. I've heard Iles accuse him of integrity – says it's why Dad will never make it to Assistant Chief.'

Harpur said: 'I do think it would be best if you left us alone for a little while, now Hazel, Jill.'

'So, why so private?' Hazel replied. 'Why?'

'This is police business,' Harpur said. 'Becky's someone else's. They have a happy household.'

'Well, we think she's really scared,' Jill said. 'But we told her you could deal with all that, Dad. Whatever.'

'Of course,' Harpur replied.

'Oh, God,' Hazel said, 'can't you? Dad, you've had bad defeats, I know. These get you down? But Iles could handle it, couldn't he? Who beats Des Iles? Shall I ring him?'

'Not for the moment. Let's see what's what.'

'What's what is she's terrified for her baby,' Hazel muttered, upset. She was fifteen, beginning to be capable of almost womanly compassion.

'We gave Rebecca Ovaltine to build her up, and the baby,' Jill said.

When the children had gone, Becky asked: 'If I left, could you help me?'

'How?'

'Well, finance, obviously. What have I got?'

'Going alone?'

'Is that tough?' she replied. 'I thought so.'

Looking at Becky, Harpur had what was for him a strange surge of non-sexual affection, even love. Or he felt almost sure it was not sexual. Hazel would probably never believe that. He was hardly moved by any thought of the coming child. He worried over Becky herself. He was intrigued by her wide, calm-seeming face, the mild grey-green eyes, the neat body, even now. Occasionally, though, the apparent calm of her features showed a restlessness and fear of boredom which must have pushed her towards Action Man, Keith Vine. Harpur had seen a thirst for kicks in the looks of lots of nice women who chose crooks. He felt part admiration, part pity, the pity because exactly what Becky chose Keith for were what made her desperate today, his push and fight and stupid spirit. Harpur dreaded to think she might get hurt. He dreaded to think the infant-to-be might get hurt, too, but that was secondary. He dreaded to think Keith might get hurt, also, and he came far-back third. In any case, did Keith still rate concern and protection, when Lamb tied him to a butchered postie?

But, of course, he said: 'It's Keith who's our responsibility, I'm afraid. And those with and dependent on Keith. *With* and dependent on, Becky. The Chief himself has to recommend aid, and I know I couldn't swing it. He loathes all grey-area stuff, and this goes beyond.'

'You wouldn't try?'

From Becky he sensed no answering affection. For her,

he was simply someone to consult, someone who had to offer help, or maybe not, like the DHSS. That made no difference to his feelings. He wondered if at last he was growing selfless, even sublime. 'I wanted Keith to leave as well,' he replied.

She picked that up instantly. 'Wanted? Don't you still? What's happened?'

You tell me. Harpur did not say it, though. He did not say anything.

'He won't go, anyway, Harpur. As your daughter said, he's changed – changed just these last few days.'

'How changed?'

She paused. 'I don't inform.'

'Of course not. Just tell me in general.'

'Optimism. Cockiness.'

And what else had she noticed? Sudden cash? Blood on his trainers? A gun? Harpur said: 'He was always pretty jaunty.'

'Now he's more. As though – as though possessed. Destiny – he thinks he's got one. In a way, inspiring.'

Yes, and why she was with him.

'All right, the odd spell when he's down,' she said, 'even scared, and he talks of France again. It never lasts. He thinks he can fight the world.'

'He's on Speed?'

'Nothing. This is just him. In a way it's wonderful, exciting, manly, I suppose. It could kill him, couldn't it, Harpur – us, all three?'

'I'll talk to him again.'

'What's the use? He thinks you're guarding your own dirty interests. You are? He doesn't hear.' She hesitated. 'He says he's left you behind.'

'Many do,' Harpur replied. 'My wife did. Keith's busy?'

She paused, weighing that one, looking for what he was asking behind it. 'As I said, optimism,' she replied.

'I like the dress,' he said.

'I had some money tucked away,' she replied at once.

'Nice.'

'So, it's gone now. That's why I'd need help, if I went.'

'Where?'

'Anywhere,' she replied. 'Nothing expensive. Not France. Just out of the target area. I can't think for three. I think for two. My parents wouldn't want me there.'

'I'll sound it with Iles and the Chief.'

'Please, be quick.'

'I know. I do know.'

She left then, and Jill and Hazel waved her off. He did not feel like being cross-questioned and went into the garden and fiddled with a rhododendron bush. They followed. 'You'll help her, Dad?' Jill asked.

'Tricky.'

Jill said: 'What I picked up was, she's living with some hood who's being hunted.'

'I wish you wouldn't use those TV words, Jill. "Hood"!'

'The question is, should his woman desert him at a time of need?' Hazel asked.

'She can't put the baby in danger,' Jill replied.

'He's one of your informants and he's menaced, is he, Dad?' Hazel asked.

Jill said: 'She seemed to think you owed her something – why stupid, vile Hazel believed you were the father.'

'*Do* you owe her something, Dad?' Hazel asked.

He did not reply.

'Yes, it's got to be that,' Jill said. 'Her man is one of your voices? To do with the terrible case that nosedived?'

'And he won't go with her?' Hazel asked. 'Some rotten business keeps him?'

'We could have an awful tragedy here,' Jill said. She, too, sounded troubled. 'Oh, please, Dad. These men who got off, they must think they can do anything. The police are a joke – I mean, more a joke than ever.'

'If you owe to her man you owe to her just as much, don't you?' Hazel asked.

'I'm not sure,' Harpur replied.

'You're sitting on all sorts we don't know about, aren't you?' Hazel asked.

'Iles often says that.'

'Iles isn't always wrong,' she replied.

'Almost never,' he said. Harpur began to think the ACC could be very right on bait. Listening to Lamb and now Becky, Harpur inevitably remade his idea of Vine. He had seemed to deserve Harpur's loyalty, and he had given it in court, and some since. But if Vine would kill for weapon cash, it put a strain. Perhaps it was fair to use him.

Harpur's daughters hung about for a while in case he disclosed more, then gave up and returned muttering to the house. He loitered. If Keith had a gun now and all this assurance, Becky was clearly right to think he would stay. Plus, there could be a possible alliance with Stan Stanfield. Stanfield was formidable. Harpur saw a chance that Claud Beyonton, Foster and Reid might get blasted by Keith and Stanley. Harpur would weep only briefly. As Iles said, what the courts failed to do villains sometimes did to one another instead, and better: a feature of the new policing, though not one to charm Lane or Civil Liberties. Somehow, the manor must be run and right given a decent chance. Oliphant Kenward Knapp himself was brilliantly removed in such strife. Gang rivalries had been happily harnessed to aid law and order, in ways trials never managed and never would, because of nobbled juries and pussyfoot judges. But Christ, he really was getting to think like Iles.

Of course, Claud and his lads might blast Keith and Stanfield, instead. That would not trouble Harpur much now, either. What did trouble him was if Becky caught a ricochet or worse. To her he felt an inescapable duty. Despite what he had just said, Lane would probably sanction funds for her to get out alone, if Harpur really put the argument. Lane had feelings. Harpur would not put the argument, though. It would involve disclosing too much. And he knew that, if she left, Keith would soon go after her and there would be no bait, no combo with Stanfield. For the moment, Keith might be gun-happy, raid-happy, kill-happy, cash-happy, but all that would fade. There was not much to him, and he had enough brain to know it. As soon as she went he would see what he had lost and go looking for her. Keith was a needful kid, a kid lusting for fatherhood.

Harpur would have to gamble with Becky, try to keep her here, so Keith stayed. It was filthy and terrifying. On the jungle drums he would let it out they had someone lined up for the post office, someone unnamed and unarrested as yet, but not Keith's age or physique. That would make him feel safer and even less like running. Harpur must try to keep a guardian eye on Becky himself, when he could. It was sure to be off-and-on only, and he had no proper reason to get issued with a gun. He had a nice little heavy-headed, very illicit metal cosh, though, which worked a treat, as long as you got close. With Claud Beyonton you might not.

Chapter 15

Keith had a call from Stanley Stanfield to suggest another meeting. This was a fine move forward, and what Keith had expected. Stanfield had limitations but he would definitely spot what was good for him. How he got to where he was – middling.

Stan said the Monty would be all right again. Keith said no way. That got Stanfield interested, obviously, but on the phone Keith did not explain, only told him it had to be somewhere else. He knew a bit more than Stanfield. He knew about Panicking Ralphy's sudden closeness to Claud and his boys. No Monty, with or without Stanfield. Often Keith knew more than others. It had made the link with Harpur. That turned out rubbish because of the court, but information was a weapon just the same, almost as good as the Makarov. Information kept him ahead. Stanfield would be wondering now what Keith knew, and this was perfect. Baffle them.

Stan had a rethink and offered an ex anti-aircraft gun post out on a hill above the city, instead. He told Keith it was always quiet there. A bit of a drag, but maybe Stanfield liked atmospherics – remoteness, the past, old cement, all that. Keith believed in learning about people's kinks. You needed to see right into anyone you would be working with, like management selection. Especially you needed it if you were dealing with a ripe piece of gorgeousness like Stanfield, so cocky cosmopolitan, plus that famed ancestor who could paint the tide.

Of course, Becky did not ask, but Keith saw she'd like to know where he was going. And he could say Stanfield again, because to her Stanfield was wonderful France. She must think really extensive research was under way, sorting out the cheeriest spot for them, where the climate was always great and night bugs in the vineyards not too noisy. He could see Becky did not believe they would ever get there, so another mention of Stanfield was a comfort to her. She deserved that. This was a very bright and loving girl. She could easily have had a career.

First thing Stanfield said was: 'I spoke to Beau Derek, and he's not against.'

'Grand, Stan. Oh, this is progress!' Christ, 'not against'. So fucking keen! Keith wished the bugger *was* against. He was dead weight.

'Depending on the detail,' Stanfield said. 'I would have brought him, but he had something else on.'

Probably a Valium banquet. You made a confidential arrangement with someone and he opens the door worldwide. Why didn't he invite his uncle, as well? 'Pity,' he said.

This spot did not look like victory. Not even Churchill could have done much with it in a speech. Grass and weeds grew everywhere, nearly swallowing the gun-site concrete and ammo truck rails. This was a place men built to win glorious survival, and now – decay. Nature was a raw, uncontrollable bastard, frightening, such as that shark in *Jaws*, munching Robert Shaw feet first regardless of shoes.

'We've got some anxieties about yourself, Keith,' Stanfield said. 'I made inquiries, obviously. Background. Not the pregnancy, we don't see that as any real problem, in fact, congratulations. But if you're in for big vengeance trouble from Claud it might be disruptive to business. Claud can be a handful. So can Foster. People get very ratty over grassing. And stay very ratty.'

'Don't worry about Claud, or any of them,' Keith replied.

Stanfield gazed up in a pretty grave mood at the sky, perhaps thinking of blitz bombers. He said: 'Oh, I remember, you've kitted yourself. That's basic. And Beau talked to Leyton Harbinger, naturally, a friend from before the Queen Mother. Don't worry, Leyton would never come right out and disclose confidentialities on clients, just guidance and hints, and the Makarov is a very decent weapon. But if you're being stalked, Keith, that can get in the way of a decent trading atmosphere.'

Christ, you would think the trade was stocks and shares. What 'decent trading atmosphere' could you have selling fixes to the hooked? 'I don't get stalked, Stanley, I stalk.' This had a real smack to it. He liked the way it came out, no thinking about it, just instinct, just the truth.

'Great, the spirit,' Stanfield said. He gave his moustache a big smooth, the smug shit. 'But all the same, Keith.'

'Stanley, we get into the fight for Kenward's complex, there's going to be resistance – stalking you call it – all round. It's a war prospect, with Claud or whoever else wants a slice. Rupert East for one. Maybe Antichrist Jessop.' Keith waved a hand over the gun emplacements, to show that wars meant hitting back, guarding your interests. 'You afraid of Claud? I can knock him over any time you like. I could have done it a day or two ago, but for an act of God.'

'And then the post office, Keith.'

That was a trick some of them loved, throw in a surprise. They learned it from the wrong end of interrogation. You kept calm, that's all. 'Which post office is that?' he replied.

Stanfield said: 'Kill a Pakistani and you get real, all-out law action these days. They've got to show ethnic. I mean, this was so small-scale, for the risk. A sensitive thing like that, Harpur could be put on himself by the Chief. Lane wants to prove he really cares.'

'Oh, *that* post office. I heard they've got someone in the frame.'

'I heard, too. But any arrest? No.'

'They pick their time, Stan.' Keith had a small walk along the parapet. God, but some bloody crudeness to bring up that post office. He strolled back. 'Harpur's no problem,' he said. 'It seems you've got all sorts who trouble you, Stan – Claud, Harpur. I know Harpur—'

'Well, of course you do. That's a worry, too.'

'He's another overrated. We could handle him. Probably he's up to his elbows grabbing for Kenward's estate, anyway. Someone else we'll have to cope with. No point in being scared of him.'

'Harpur involved?' That seemed to shake Stanfield. Another advance.

'Believe me,' Keith replied. 'Harpur, Iles. Plus Panicking.'

'Well, Panicking, yes, you'd expect that. And possibly Iles. But Harpur?'

'I tell you I know him. They see what they think is easy income, fast gain. Don't we all?' He had a laugh, a good, solid laugh, to show this jerk he could not shove Keith Vine off his perch – still able to get a giggle at himself. He felt a bit like a warrior, up on this parapet. From here, the city looked so warm and legs open, ready for taking. Maybe this spot could grow on you. 'Panicking's in with Claud.'

'Well, yes,' Stanfield said.

Of course, this one would never show twice in one day he did not know something. Why choose the Monty for a meeting, then, if he'd heard about Ember? He was pathetic, but humour him. Let's keep his ego in one piece or he would be useless, more useless. 'You worry about me, Stan, I worry about you. That's how it's always going to be, building a confederation, give and take. I mean, you nibbling at Jack Lamb's girl. Don't tell me you never heard Lamb might talk to Harpur. How else do you think that art business gets away with so much?'

'All sorts talk to Harpur, Keith. Like I say, we worry over that connection.'

'Many might see a very dodgy link there, Stan – you to the girl to Lamb to Harpur. Myself, no, not troubled. You're entitled. I would have perfect faith: someone of your experience, Stan, could be fucking a tremendous girl on a totally regular basis, a true and mature relationship, yet only whispering very select material in her ear, mainly love talk. But then again, you're anxious about Claud coming after me. I could be anxious about Lamb coming after you, in person I mean, not just tips to Harpur. Or some paid pistol. Lamb's getting old, Stan. He's rich, yes, but he won't be pulling girls like Helen Surtees much longer. Hair going, teeth going, dong going, probably. You could look very dangerous to him, I mean the moustache and lively Continental flavour, plus that notable forebear. Lamb would want to do something final, maybe.'

Stan climbed up on to the parapet alongside Keith and they both gazed down at the city. 'I think we could work together, all the same,' Stanfield said.

'Sure of it.'

'And Beau will accept anything I agree. He's so good like that.'

'Sensational.'

'When you said you nearly took out Claud, what did – ?'

'An interception, but then a factor that should never have been there.'

Stanfield gave a forgiving few nods. 'My feeling is, we shouldn't try anything like that just now. Later, we might have to, you're right, Keith. Now, while we're getting things set up, getting our system running, contacts made, we need some calm. Obviously, if he came after you, we'd have to deal with him. But not taking things to him for now. This might go against the grain, Keith, and I do understand. I've always liked a quiet opening, though, always found it works.'

'This was an impulse,' Keith replied, 'trying to turn things around.'

'And natural. Well, in a way, all credit. This is guts, this is steel,' Stanfield replied. 'But—'

'I see your thinking, Stan.' The smug shit.

Chapter 16

Mrs Lamb, over on her yearly visit from the States, said: 'You could follow her, Jack.'

'Mother, I'm not—'

'Or get someone to follow her. You know the people. You know people could do anything. I've seen some. Just anything, Jack.'

'Look, I'd rather if—'

'I know, I know, private, a man and his woman. So, I just watch you suffer? That's motherhood?'

'It could sort itself out,' Lamb replied. His mother saw too much too fast, and always had. Jack loved her and knew she had given him most of his brains and energy. All the same, she could push too hard.

'The man younger than you?' she asked. She was stretched out on a chesterfield in one of those terrible dresses. She had money but bought stuff like that, as some sort of general insult to the world. Now and then he would give her an expensive and nice creation and never saw her wear it. 'Well, sure, younger than you. Every time I visit you look older, Jack. What I mean, time before last, older than Nixon. Last time, older than Reagan. Now, older than Nancy. You're not fifty. Not forty-eight. Fresher faces on TV from Parliament.'

'I shouldn't have told you.'

'Jack, I'd smell it.'

Yes. 'Helen's so interested in everyone, enthusiastic. Mother, she makes friends fast, you see. So wonderfully open. That's lovely in her. Maybe it's friendship only. Probably. I can't object to that.'

'Open, yeah. Jack, for Chrissake, this is a girl of nineteen, blood up. She's destroying you. He a crook? Naturally. Who else do you know – crooks, police?' She twisted her head around to stare at him, where he stood gazing from the French windows. 'How about this cop who came here once – looks like Rocky Marciano, but fair.'

'Harpur.'

'You get on all right with him, don't you? That's how it looked. More'n all right? So, can't Mr Cop Harpur get this crook dungeoned till she's grey, skin-dead? By then you wouldn't be interested neither. He could take her over when released. Anything would look good to him in, say, the year 2020. Harpur owes you? How it also looked.' Mrs Lamb's eyes darkened. She swung her legs down and sat up. 'Or, now wait a minute, Jesus, yes – he's not the one screwing her, the cop? That badge, way in anywhere, they think. Jack, didn't I tell you on your twenty-first, never, never leave police alone in a room with a woman or portable antiques? But I thought he had some student kid, friend of Helen.'

'Here she is now. You'll be careful?'

They were in the drawing room of Lamb's place, Darien, and he watched Helen's Maestro emerge crackling over the gravel from the long, tree-bordered drive and pull in at the front door. Stanfield could give her something like this? Ever?

His mother said: 'I don't want you brought down, Jack. A woman treats you like shit – anything's better than that. Anything, you hear? That goes to my soul.'

'It's not going to happen.'

She grinned suddenly and smacked her thin thigh under the thin material with her thin fingers. 'You've got something decisive lined up already? Great? Of course, I should have known. Jack Lamb is still Jack Lamb. Who will you go for, her or him? Well, Helen darling, I just said to Jack, such a sway and swing in your step, everybody could see you're a dancer.'

'Just very amateur.' Helen skipped forward into the room past the Hockney, put her arm around Mrs Lamb's shoulders and kissed her twice, once on the temple, once on the cheek. Lamb saw his mother's nostrils widen, like doing what she just said, sniffing out betrayal.

Then, when Helen switched to him, and pulled his head down so she could kiss him too in the same spots, he found he wanted his mouth on her lips, to see if she tasted of someone else. Not just someone else, still Stanley. She smelled only of herself, that wonderful clean, youngish, unperfumed smell of warm flesh, with perhaps far off the hint of a very basic pungent soap, even Lifebuoy. He sat down and she held him, as she had held Mrs Lamb, with an arm around his shoulders. He knew his mother would spot how much that meant to him: to be gripped as if Helen needed him the way he needed her. His mother would pity him for it.

She would look at Helen and see a racy, sexy kid tiring of him, questing elsewhere, searching for glamour, not security, but cleverly sticking with the security, too, so far. His mother might even understand that, but not forgive. She was telling him he had to stop it somehow. Anyhow. And he, when he looked at Helen, also saw a kid, a kid who kept him together. Thanks to Helen, this country house and the money he piled up in the art game and otherwise meant something good. And thanks to Helen the ways he piled it up seemed more or less all right, because it bought them a life she liked, and she never objected. If it pleased her, it pleased Lamb. Or, at least until now it bought them a life she liked.

Of course, she did not have an account in detail of how he put his wealth together, but this was a bright child who saw what made the world turn. It tore him to think she might go, and at his age such damage left you for ever sick and sinking, too swamped by defeat to surface again. For her to go at all would be bad enough, but to go to somebody else – that would wipe him out. No, no, not just somebody else: to Stan and his petty, shaky, perilous villain life. Jack almost wept.

So, by his own route, he reached the same place as his mother. He had to stop this, somehow and anyhow. Already Harpur had failed once to do it in the way she suggested, the jail way. Lamb decided there was no need to tell her how he would deal with it. He might fail again. But, as his mother had mentioned, Jack Lamb was in touch with all sorts of quite handy people. And he could be quite handy himself at a push. This was a push.

Chapter 17

The ACC said he absolutely craved one of their regular saunters to the Monty on a terrorizing trip, to show Panicking's villain clientèle that Harpur and Iles had not been beaten.

'But we *have* been beaten, sir.'

'Why it's necessary, cunt,' the Assistant Chief replied. 'Tonight, Harpur.'

They were in Iles's room, waiting for Lane to join them. This was how the Chief usually preferred conferences: away from his own suite, to suggest modesty and the informal. When he arrived, Lane was in shirtsleeves with brownish tie pulled down and white-ish collar part open. He had on baggy, khaki-ish socks and was shoeless. When in civvies, he generally dressed along these lines, also for informality: his answer to those who wanted Chief Constables to be ex-military officers, as in the past. Lane's proud scruffiness signalled what he often stated, that police were for ever civilian and of their community. Watching him shuffle humbly along a corridor one day, Iles had said: 'Whichever community Lane and you other fucking coolies belong to, Harpur, count me out.'

Iles stood immediately and smiled a grand welcome: 'Here *is* the Chief, Col. Now, we can take a grip on our worst problems.'

Lane sat down. 'This boy Keith Vine, Colin's informant. I'm still waiting for a request to fix him up elsewhere.'

Iles said: 'This one's a—'

'I want him away from here, Desmond,' the Chief replied. 'Has the situation been clearly put to Vine, Colin? I mean, the uncontrollable dangers, and then, on the other side, what we can offer to ensure his safe new life – are in fact required and eager to offer?' His voice raced and sang to match this generosity, and because he visualized a spell of peace once Keith Vine was gone. 'Possibly I should see him myself. Some of these people seem unaware how deep the hate for grasses goes. Especially, for some reason, grasses who fail.'

Iles said: 'Because bastards who should be inside for ever are out and go hunting.'

'He knows his position, sir,' Harpur told Lane.

'Colin thinks Vine might decide to take our offer at any time.'

Lane stared about the room as though for aid, obviously wondering if he was once more up against an accomplished, foul alliance which would lie to him and edit and omit for shady purposes. The Chief had limited cleverness and was not strong. Nobody was clever enough or strong against Iles. The ACC used the enhanced insights and extra power of obsession. He sat down again at his desk, rarely bothering to look at Lane. Instead, Iles gazed critically but affectionately now and then into the big mirror alongside his desk, meant for checking uniform.

One of those thin, red lines of anger or frustration or dread suddenly snaked across Lane's beige complexion again. 'Clearly, what I could not tolerate, Desmond, Colin, is this lad being used as bait.'

Iles pulled a pad towards him. He spoke as he made a note. *Intolerable should be used as bait.* He laughed as if uneasily. 'I've written that down, sir, because I can see it is something on which you're set. Yet I'm afraid I do not understand what it means. Colin, do you? *As bait.*'

Iles did like to be answered. Harpur said to the Chief: 'This is an interesting analysis, sir.'

'Exactly,' Iles said. 'Analysis. Sometimes, sir, when you expound a case or situation, I'm afraid I feel short of street savvy. And you, Col?'

'A fresh mind looking at these things will often come up with a thought not considered by those working closer to the matter,' Harpur proffered.

Iles rapped the desk fiercely with the side of his gold propelling pencil. 'You've hit it, Col. Again. That's why these meetings are so nutritious, sir. The unencumbered overview.'

Lane let it go on. Then he said: 'Bait, yes. This boy grassed and can probably be traced despite all our brick-walling in court, so it's likely someone will come after him, perhaps more than one. This means he would be a target, but so might the pursuit be, if, say we were waiting to settle an account missed earlier.' He stared at the ACC. 'I.e., bait.'

'My God, sir,' Iles replied.

'You see why I say intolerable?' the Chief asked.

'My God, sir,' Iles replied.

'Endless, endless, endless,' Lane muttered. 'An appalling cycle. Horton and McCallion are killed by competitors for Knapp's plums, so their friend Vine seeks revenge by informing on those he thought did it.'

'Did it,' Iles replied.

'Those he tried to punish want revenge on *him*, and can deduce who he is. Then, if those themselves are made targets, their friends will come later for vengeance in their turn.'

'Happily, those three murderous shits have no friends,' Iles replied.

'This is anarchy,' Lane said. 'I will not permit incitement to chaos, Desmond.'

Iles repeated and wrote this phrase.

Always the Chief was frantically alert for early symptoms of impending cataclysm and the enduring victory of lawlessness and evil. Lane's special fear was that the disaster would begin in this domain through his error or neglect or blindness, before marching on to eat the cosmos. He was a good Catholic with the customary load of potential and present guilt. His anguish had been one factor that pushed him into the recent breakdown, though only a very minor cause compared with Iles. The Chief's head dropped for a few seconds now, his chin resting on the brown tie. Yet he had been looking very passable since his return from sick-leave.

Iles said: 'Chaos? I'd say Claud Beyonton skipping free and chortling is chaos.'

Harpur spoke to Lane: 'People like Keith Vine – they have binding ties here, sir. Often they're afraid of new environments. We've had this trouble with grasses before. Inertia.'

'You know as fact Claud and the rest will come for him, don't you?' the Chief replied. His voice had both rage and weariness. At any time, he might slip again into crippling depression. 'You count on it, plan for it.' He seemed to be speaking to both of them, speaking to a conspiracy. Lane had fine, old-world values and Iles once said he would be the life and soul of an Eventide Home.

'I've asked Col to give him some protection for the time being,' the ACC replied.

'But that's what I mean,' Lane said. 'Vine draws revenge and we target the avengers.'

'So, do I leave the bugger wide open, sir?' Iles asked. 'Let me know if that's what you wish. Or your wife.' He whispered the last words, but Lane's head rose sharply. 'A man's life,' Iles said, as though repeating the phrase at full voice.

Possibly the ACC would be shocked to hear Vine was already wide open, unguarded because Harpur had nobody good enough to do it. 'Keith's mentioned France,' Harpur said. 'It might take a while for him to finalize.'

'Isn't there a woman, and a little one on the way?' Lane asked.

'Probably little, yes, sir,' Iles replied.

Lane said: 'Doesn't Vine see what he's doing – putting three at peril? My God. On my patch.' He pulled himself around, grew decisive. 'Look, would she leave without Keith, Colin? I'd be prepared to finance that. Oh, yes, for two reasons. First and paramount, her own and the child's safety. Second, some men are dependent on women and, if his partner went, there must be a chance Keith would follow. Not just a matter of the woman, after all. Fatherhood is a great pull, you know.'

Iles said: 'Keith Vine is—'

'How do you see it, Colin?' the Chief asked. 'Would the woman go alone, in the first instance?'

Iles said: 'Are we entitled to put them asunder? I know you have an abiding sense of the sanctity of Family, sir. Think of cruelly segregated workhouses last century.'

'How do you see it, Colin?' the Chief asked. 'Would the woman go alone, in the first instance, if we put money her way?'

'As Mr Iles says, this is a tricky one, sir,' Harpur replied.

'Ask her,' Lane replied. 'Or then again, I would be prepared to talk to her myself.'

'This is a remarkable yet typically caring offer, sir, if I may say,' Iles replied.

'Nothing at all. Please see the urgency, Desmond. How would I feel, we feel, if she were gunned down here in her state?' Lane asked. 'How would we *look*? Do I provide the killing fields? We?'

In the car on their way to the Monty that night, Iles said: ' "The killing fields." His vocab's only ten years out of date. Obviously, we don't let either of those two anywhere near His Serene Tenderness, Harpur. I revere that man. Sweet as a wreath. Defeat adores him and for ever holds his hand. You've talked to the woman?'

'Of course.'

'She wants money to go?'

'Of course.'

'You told her it's probably not on?'

'Of course.'

'Best leave it like that, wouldn't you say, Harpur?'

'I worry about her.'

'Nice. We all worry, but there's a realm to be run, to be saved. The Chief's right and, if she went, Keith would follow. We can't have that. Not at this stage.'

'This is the stage when they might get hit, once they think they've identified him. Anger's still up.'

'Yes, a chance of doing Claud and so on any day now.' Briefly, he hummed an ecstatic ditty. 'Remember those punching-the-air, victory pics of them on the court steps after they got off? Ever since, I see the bastards vivid in my dreams, even displacing Monroe's tits in *Some Like It Hot*.'

'Sir, this woman, Becky, is entirely outside all this, yet in peril. I really do—'

Harpur was driving and Iles gently touched his arm in a comforting and very comradely fashion: 'You want me to make it an outright order that you're not to talk to her yet, do you Harpur, you snivelling, retarded jerk, so your delicious conscience can stay intact even if she's damaged?'

'Fuck your orders. I could go to Lane and get different.'

'Fair, Col. But you wouldn't, would you? Even for you that would be a scum act.'

'I'm messing about with three lives, one we owe a lot to, two innocent.'

'It's called policing, Harpur.'

'I—'

'You flopped in court. We require confrontation. Keith and the girl are the route.'

Harpur decided he would tell Becky about Lane's offer to her. She had to be protected.

Iles led into the Monty beaming, glaring about, his walk a war lord's stride despite everything. As always when Iles turned up, there was an immediate drop in noise.

Talk and laughter stopped for a few seconds, the pool games went into pause. You could hear the words of the jukebox lyrics. Then things resumed. Harpur thought they resumed slightly quicker than they used to. He also thought members looked less worried than they used to by his and Iles's arrival. Claud's triumph brought spin-off bits of bravery and defiance all round. Iles knew these had to be faced and squashed fast or they would become immovable. Lane would not do it, could not do it, might not see it as vital or even proper. Perhaps he was right. Iles would relish the role.

Beyonton, Foster and Reid were in the club, seated at a table with Foster's Deloraine and what seemed to be a couple of very young tarts in that kind of clothes. Iles immediately walked over to them all. 'Well, here's a treat,' he cried. 'Harpur's so eager to join you. Do you mind?' With noisy eagerness, he brought chairs and made places for himself and Harpur between Foster and Deloraine. 'You two sweet girls, Avis, Cheryl, one knows from way back, of course. Splendid to see you again, and still looking so hale yet sensitive. And then Claud and Harry and Gerry familiar from photographs and what I've read. I feel as if I know you lads myself – Claud with his garments and so on. Plus,' he turned excitedly to his left: 'You *have* to be Deloraine. Yes? Those lips! Harpur's wonderfully right about them, particularly the upper.'

Deloraine said with a fine smile to the ACC: 'Obviously, these boys hate you and Harpur through and through, and especially Claud does, but you don't look as bad as I expected, Iles. Nearly refined and human. Quite intelligent. I believe you'd admit people are entitled to a life.'

'Which people are those, Deloraine?' Iles replied.

'Well, Claud, Harry and Gerry, naturally.'

'Oh, I certainly wouldn't go that far,' Iles said. ' "A life"? Couldn't you think of something else, something more likely and less of a public nuisance?' Ember approached. 'Bravo,' Iles cried. 'Drinks all round, Ralphy. Armagnac for my friends here? Harpur the usual pleb mix, gin and cider. Myself, a nice port and lemon. You know these folk, Ralphy? Well, of course you do, you know all your members personally right down to the dregs. It's friendliness that gives the Monty its wholesome flavour. The freedom party was here, yes? We missed that, didn't we, Harpur, but one hears tell. The lawyers, too? They damn well deserved it. Charlie Couzel QC embodies that great principle of British law: everyone is innocent until proved guilty, especially the guilty. I would go to the stake denying rumours he and the judge fuck each other turn and turn about. What will you be doing now, Claudy? Ralph, do they discuss these things with you at all, you sage old head? Girls, one thing about Ralphy, he's not just a face behind a bar. Well, you'll know there's much more to him, I expect. This is a figure with many enterprises and devoted women admirers. He's doing a university degree, and has potent letters in the local press. Such a strength to those who know him.'

'And how's Mrs Iles?' Ember replied. He seemed to aim the question at both the ACC and Harpur as if not sure who could answer best. Well, yes, there had been something with Sarah Iles a while ago. Ember went back to bring the drinks.

Reid said in a big, passionate voice: 'Iles, you think nothing, nothing of the liberty of the individual, nor does your snooping sidekick. Wrongly arraigned and foully traduced, we could be languishing now in captivity, merely to further your harsh career.'

'We're thinking of going for wrongful arrest, Iles,' Beyonton said.

'This is harassment now,' Foster said, 'crowding us, the conversation. Remarks about Del's lips. This is a girl on a quiet evening out.'

Ember brought drinks.

Reid said: 'We're entitled to our dignity, aren't we, to simple respect and honour as men living out their days as best they can?'

'So why don't you piss off from our table, Iles?'

Beyonton said. 'You're the past. And Harpur even more.'

Harpur thought it might be an idea to leave them to it, but Iles was obviously settling down for the evening, full of joyous savagery.

'Who you seeing these days, nights, Desy?' Cheryl asked. She sounded hurt. 'Not us. I said to Avis last week, maybe some executive sickness, or gone gay – that eternal search for novelty.'

'Desy had such a lovely, impetuous way with cash, yet I will not believe he's into rackets,' Avis sighed to Reid. 'Twosomes, threesomes, just the same.'

Looking worried, Cheryl said to Claud: 'There's something really evil between you boys and Desy. I can feel it, nearly touch it. I heard Deloraine say hate. But who would hate Desy? Who *could*?'

'What shall we toast?' Iles replied. He stood, port and lemon held high. Harpur and all the others stayed seated. The ACC said: 'Ladies and gentlemen, I give you the—'

He did not complete it, because the glass was suddenly struck from his hand and flew across the table spattering Beyonton's great suede jacket and tasselled purple shirt. A woman screamed: 'It's what I thought if I came here. Bloody police and killers drinking together, sharing our territories and women.'

Harpur recognized Josh McCallion's untidy widow, Dorothy.

'What you drinking to then, Iles?' she said. 'Some swag divide between the lot of you? Or the classic way Harpur scuppered the trial by silence and got your damn mates off?'

She was about fifty, stout and worn-looking, her grey hair anyhow, her clothes dismal. She must have come into the club without being noticed. Ember was still standing near the table and said: 'Madam, I don't know who you are, but I cannot tolerate such behaviour in the Monty. You have no right here. I will not have bona fide members disturbed. Please leave at once.' He was close to her and, putting his tray on the table, turned to grab her arm. She threw him off and stepped towards Beyonton, plump fists raised. 'Smirking, sodding murderer,' she yelled. 'You can beat or buy these two, but not me.'

Beyonton stood swiftly, grinning nor smirking, and stretching out an arm grabbed her by the throat, easily keeping her off. Harpur jumped up and broke Beyonton's grip. 'Don't you touch me, corrupt bastard,' she shouted at Harpur. He held her back, as gently as he could. Beyonton sat down again, still grinning, and mopped at the wine on his clothes with a handkerchief.

Deloraine also stood and said: 'But what's the trouble with this lady? What's upset her?'

Harpur muttered: 'Please, this isn't the way, Mrs McCallion.'

'What *is* the way?' she muttered. 'Is there a way?' Her body relaxed suddenly and she gave up trying to get at Beyonton, fight gone. 'Your way? Is there nobody to help us any longer?'

Harpur thought he would not speak to Becky about Lane's offer after all. The bait project was vital.

Beyonton said: 'Look, you two alleged police saw what happened, but I'm not going to make trouble for the scraggy old thing. Just get rid of her, Ralphy. And make sure she never comes back in, or I don't know what.' His mouse-face had changed to a kind of snarl, a mouse kind.

Reid went on: 'We believe in generosity, the wider view. Yet we ask again, is it now a fact that friends cannot go for a quiet drink without these gross and insulting incidents? Where are the sound old simplicities of life?'

Conversation in the club had fallen again, but it now resumed as Ember led Mrs McCallion towards the door. By Monty standards the disturbance had been minor. Mrs McCallion's head was bent forward and Harpur thought she must be quietly weeping. Ember left her in the middle of the floor and went to the bar. He poured a big brandy and took it over. They sat together on a bench near the

109

door until she had finished it. Ember seemed to talk consolingly. Then she left.

Foster said: 'No class there. Just like Josh. Abject. Pitiful.'

Iles had sat down and Ember brought him another port and lemon. 'She seemed to have it in for you, Claud,' the ACC said. 'I don't know why that would be, nice little features like yours.'

'She despises you, Iles,' Foster said. 'And Harpur. You injured her somehow? Failed her?'

'I'm used to contempt,' the ACC replied.

'Don't put yourself down always, Desy,' Avril cried. 'Almost all the younger girls see you as a total gent and a turn-on.'

'Oh, which don't?' Iles replied.

As they were driving back, the ACC said: 'I had a look at that post office slaughter scene, talked to one or two people in the shops, and there are some fragmentary descriptions about. Francis Garland handling it? Cock imperatives keep his eyes steamed, you know, Harpur, and he misses things. I don't believe he's reached the same witnesses. I'd say it sounds like Keith Vine. He was masked, but the physique. You knew this? Obviously. He'd be financing himself for a weapon to contest Kenward's riches and pay off the hire. After a shooting like that and a bit of a collection he'll be on a marvellous high and totally immovable for now. The girl wearing anything new lately? He'd try to keep her happy here. Probably we could force Leyton to put us in the picture on the guns, if we wanted to be put in the picture, but I agree with you. We keep Keith in play for now. What use, bait locked away? Was it you who spread the tale about someone older, bigger, to soothe him? Smart. Sometimes I think you're wasted in my shadow, Col. But who'd throttle your damned humaneness if it wasn't Des Iles?'

'I'm working on it myself,' Harpur replied.

'It disfigures you, Col, and you can't afford disfigurement on top of your looks.'

Chapter 18

The four of them were in Claud's Saab again, on their way for a repeat look at a bank cash collection by armoured van. Ember wanted to soak up more geography and get another feel of the street under his shoes and theirs. Claud drove, wearing a different, pinstripe, mouse-tycoon suit, with Ember alongside him, Reid and Harry Foster in the back. It was definitely reconnaissance only again today, though Ember had an idea that at least Claud and Foster carried something. Perhaps they always did. They were the sort, and it was the way the whole world went now, not just the States.

The blue and white security van appeared ahead out of a side-street on its way to the bank, and Ember told Claud to let his speed fall, so they would stay far behind. Guards spotted everything and reported in for the record. Of course, Ember would not be using the Saab in the raid, but police would check all registrations noted for months back, and if they found Claud they found every-one. The van varied its route each week. That did not matter much. It would always arrive at the bank. It varied its time, too, but never more than ten minutes each side of 11 a.m. This week it was 10.50, next it would be 11.10, the week after 11.00, then back to 10.50.

Claud and the other two regarded Ember as a living wizard for this bit of rock-bottom research. He regarded *them* as – well, bold enough and very hard, and very hard for police to deal with since the acquittals. Fire-proof, yes.

This was a good, give-and-take alliance. These three boys claimed they had been on very fruitful money raids before, but Ember wondered. His information said they knew small-time drug pushing, not much else. He had to get them really acquainted with an armoured vehicle and the pavement distance between it and the bank doors, and the way the guards covered that distance with the bags, one carrying money, the other with his hands and arms free for the truncheon in his belt holster.

Ember did a bit of a traffic survey as they drove. Although he distrusted deep, rigid planning, he did need to breathe the air of a job location before the day. He liked anyone working with him to breathe it too, especially nobody jerks like these three. God, but the atmosphere in this car took him back. There was grand tension and a feel of power – the sense that next week they could stand on a pavement and take a stack of money from men who were supposed to stop raiders taking it, and who had been trained to stop raiders taking it, but who would not have a hope, if it all went right.

The traffic flow was good – not enough to slow them, but adequate to keep them unnoticed. Obviously, you could never rely completely on the flow being the same, but he had done a few counts around 11 a.m., and it seemed pretty constant. There was a nice lack of really bulky stuff which might have been pulled across to make a roadblock if some driver saw the attack and went public-spirited. A few stupid sods still did, despite everything. This raid should be the only time the four of them would need to do heavy work. Good Christ, he was going to be BA soon, with Religious Knowledge modules in the degree, and he could not go around cracking money vans and guards then. Once they'd bought the first stock with this take, the business funded itself, unless partners drank or sniffed or motorized or womanized/jewellerized the profits.

But nobody could take over Oliphant Kenward

Knapp's juicy kingdom without weighty cash up front to buy the first major supply, and Ember had convinced Claud and the other two it must be bank transit funds. This work was natural to him. Claud and his lads could not argue against, anyway, because they did not know enough. Miniature people. Why they had asked him in. They wanted Ember to transform them, jack them up to the grandeur of prime operators he'd worked with in the unmatchable past. Maybe they also thought he was so big he could get credit from suppliers, so capital would not be needed until their business raised its own.

But Ember never gave guarantees, never put his skin in hock. Possibly they even hoped he'd bankroll the new business. Never would he do that either, though, even if he had enough. All the wealth he had cornered in his bright careers he regarded as not just his but his wife's and daughters', plus a slice for Christine Tranter, of course, easily his most valued girlfriend. Investing in a dirty, dodgy, high-return enterprise would be gross betrayal of Margaret, the children and Christine. He ignored hints from Claud about 'a float' and suggested the bank collection instead.

The van did all the usual speed tricks, accelerating suddenly, slowing suddenly, checking whether anything tried to keep pace. Claud stayed steady. He had a lot of low-calibre sense, this vermin-face. In fact, Ember thought the three of them undeniably brilliant last night at the Monty. That incident with McCallion's widow could have put the business plan right back, yet it was kept tolerable, and as soon as Iles and Harpur left, Ember congratulated them. They would cherish any praise from him. 'Beautiful control, Claud. We mustn't let anything disturb things now.' He was really talking about any crazy vengeance hunt for the grass who nearly sold them, not that club fracas, but did they understand? Later, he ran the event through in his head to make sure nothing that happened told Harpur and Iles he was in with Claud. It seemed all

right. He had behaved through-and-through pot-boy –
how that sod Iles liked to see him.

The van pulled in on double yellows at the bank and
Claud took them past at a nice, unnoticeable pace. Sometimes, Ember thought he had outgrown this kind of work
and its street thrills. Maybe the club and new knowledge
at university were enough. Then a trip like today's would
suddenly tell him he had been starving himself. How could
he get one of his panics in the club or a lecture room?
And he always needed the threat of that. Fright to him
meant he was living full out, and those breakdowns were
his core, like a backbone or prayer. On top, there was the
matter of boosting income to meet brutal new costs. After
his daughter, Venetia, showed an unbreakable appetite
for older, villainous men, he had sent her to a finishing
school in France. It bemused him that a child of his should
be like this at fifteen, after her upbringing. You had to
shovel the francs out for nun-warders and ankle irons.
And now the needs of this business on top.

As they passed the bank, Ember and Reid, on the
nearside of the Saab, turned their heads inwards to give
no profiles and to obscure Claud and Harry Foster. None
of them looked at the van. Ember had coached them
in that. They would drive on and park, then walk back
separately to resee the scene and put extra bits of it in
their memories. There would be just time. It was the kind
of routine Ember had done so often before. This troupe
were lucky to get him, and knew it. From him they could
learn not just the detail of a raid, but generalship and
strategy.

The strategy was cash. You bought your opening supplies bulk for cash, you put them on the street in cash
through a long string of little-life pushers, who bought
from you in cash. What you took in naturally added up
to more cash than you bought for, and then you went
back with most of the takings for new bulk supplies and
so on. By then the business was unstoppable, no advertis-

ing costs, no heavy plant or pensions for the workers. At that stage you might rate credit, but cash remained the true foundation.

So, to start, you needed a decent pile of bills, and finding this sort of funds meant either a money van, or do the bank itself. Funds on the move were easier: no barricade over the bank counter to pass or reinforced doors. This would be two or three men in flak jackets and crash helmets, carrying nothing saucier than sticks, and ready for taking if you were quick and ruthless.

In the Saab now, as they parked, Ember wiped some sweat from his upper lip with two fingers. The thought of ruthlessness had produced a tiny tremor. Ruthlessness he could fall down on. It was how his cruel nickname began, Panicking Ralph or even Panicking Ralphy. He knew people said there were men doing endless time and one in a wheelchair because Panicking had come apart on some job, jobs. This was vindictiveness, envy, lies. In any case, this small shiver in the Saab was nothing like one of his full collapses, only a novice sweat. His legs felt fine. To Claud, Harry and Gerry he would look really majestic, a chieftain, as he stepped from the car and set off alone walking back to the bank. The others would do the same. They expected resolute, battle-proved leadership from him, and by Christ they could totally count on it most likely.

Strolling here was a risk. If you ran a club, a lot of people knew your face. People at the university knew his face, too – students, staff. But his face would not be on show when they did the job. They would mask for that. All anyone who recognized him now would see was Ralph Ember out walking in a part of the city far from the Monty. So what? This could be his bank. Of course, there might be spotter cameras filming pedestrians non-stop. Police would go through that record, too. This was one reason they had to keep apart. Even that could be a hazard. Those three were known as a unit. Naturally they were, they'd trio'd at the bottom of the heap for years, and then reached court together for double murder. It might tell a tale if they were spotted on film, obviously steering clear of one another, and all parading near a bank when interesting bagged cash was crossing the pavement.

He glanced behind and saw them well strung-out. It might work. He continued on, crossed the road and went back on the other pavement. The three remained separated, Reid on Ember's side of the road. Although this was all new for these lads, they had listened to what he said and did it perfectly. They were infants but they could grow. The more he saw of them, the more sure he felt right to tolerate them for a while in partnership. Even if they tried nailing the grass shortly, they could probably manage it all right, and not involve him. True, they had almost fucked up on Alby and Josh McCallion, but there would be no informant nearly to sink them this time.

Back in the Saab they discussed the sights. Harry loved it that the guards seemed such easy meat, so old and fat. Ember could have said it might be different guards on the day, and could have said that even someone old and fat might turn out brave and deeply perilous. That he had seen before. He let it go now, though, to help morale. If they felt happy they might do it all the better. Also, some of their confidence would reach him, help settle any of those sudden drops into crippling terror. That's how teams operated: propped one another, not just in the raid, but through the run-up.

Ember said they all had to stay in one place for two days and nights before, to strengthen team solidity. Of course, he never let outright business activity touch the club, and would not have them in the Monty flat, although it was unused now. And he certainly could not let them into his home, alongside his wife and other daughter, Fay. Claud Beyonton at Low Pastures! Jesus. Claud said he was alone at present and invited them to his place, but Ember objected. To him, Beyonton looked a target: the

116

smart-arse clothes, his stunted swagger, the poison. It could be that mad sod Iles, it could be relatives of Alby and Josh, it could be the little grass, trying defence by attack. Someone talented might wipe out all four of them as they innocently slept. Then, Harry Foster's place was no good because he had Deloraine living with him. Foster said she would never talk, but Ember hated women around the night before a task, and he did not believe Foster, anyway, because they all talked if something turned them nasty, and almost anything could. He must remember Deloraine for an empty night in the vacation. She was friendly.

It had to be Reid's dump for their gang nest. The place was down off Valencia Esplanade, and not all that far from where Alby and Josh were found. There was no woman with him at present, either, and this was an area where people came and went and nobody wanted to know. Gerry had a furnished flat in one of the big, old houses not quite ready for demolition, plenty of uncleaned rooms, plenty of shattered beds. It was only two nights.

Chapter 19

Keith Vine could never understand friends who told him they went off their women when they were pregnant. He thought Becky looked great, and he wanted her as much as ever, or more. That shiny mound above the other furry mound was a real turn-on. You could see sex had a meaning. Of course, you knew that before, but now you could feel this while you were actually doing it, and it was great. When he heard about Harpur having it off they reckoned with some student only for the sake of it, or Iles going to young tarts although married, it seemed to Vine they were just hogs missing the thorough joy, and he would have thought this even if they were not top police. They were not seeking the in-depth experience that God had meant. Pussies were fine, but pussies just as pussies were not the be-all and end-all, and it was the same with boobs. Boobs, which were only playthings and nibble-things before, you could tell now were going to be very useful soon, life-support items each. Yes, you knew that before, too, but now you could watch the lovely change: they seemed to get a different character, rounder, even more welcoming, the nipples pointing so blunt and pink and brave to the future. Hope was what tits said. He found it nearly impossible to imagine her damaged or killed, because she and what she had were so obviously a part of the next century. They had to be there.

This was why he considered it a true privilege to fuck someone in Becky's state, and he would occasionally almost weep with emotion. He could not add anything now to the birth, it was all sealed up and lively in there, floating in its potential and the fluid, but these were moments when glorious motherhood gave herself to a man just for love between the two of them. It might even be extra love, she to him for placing the child, he to her for niching and nourishing it for him. They were more bound than ever, and this comforted and excited him at the same time. To go into her under the bulge was like registering with the human race's endless renewal knack, and a dick should show pride. If she had not tired quicker now, he would have had her all night. Not this night, though, because he was seeing Stanfield again at around eleven out at some foreshore defence blockhouse. Always military. It might be that trenches moustache.

The table-lamp was on. 'So beautiful,' he said in bed, touching her shoulders and arms, just drawing his hand over them very lightly, like a skimming pebble. That was the thing – all her skin seemed warmer and sweeter, more unmistakably a woman's. Until this, he might have been a bit like Harpur and Iles and many others himself, he had to admit, just sex-questing, and his reverence for Becky was even greater because she had shown him how narrow and barren his outlook was then. 'I will always cherish you and look after you and the child, Becky.'

She touched his shoulders and arms, too, like they were giving some sort of silent greeting-signs the way Red Indians did. It was nice, yet she seemed sad. Although her breasts were bonny and full of fight and promise, her face was full of worry. He realized he could not tell her again that the meeting with Stanfield was another session on France, not so late. Perhaps he'd say it was some different contact. She did not cry, nothing gross like that, just stared up past him at the picture rail while still smoothing the tops of his arms. He had heard of the blues after sex but this was more. And he knew what obviously. He considered her bloody selfish to be going over all that again in her head after such lovemaking, with himself making every allowance for her waist. If she started on about moving abroad, he would get up soon and go to see Stanfield. 'Provide, provide, provide, that's what I have to do now, Becky, and I do not regard it as just a duty, it's a real theme to life. You and it deserve everything.'

The words came out like singing and he could feel himself hardening up once more, sweetly. There would be no time for that again now, though. This was a crux meeting with Stan. Stanfield believed himself Mr Almighty and would notice lateness. You had to kowtow to the prat. Tonight Keith must talk money, money in detail, and he did not want to start wrong by making Stanfield wait. Could Stan bankroll the first load, or if not, could he use his name and aura to get credit? Why else did he think Keith had picked him? With someone so in love with himself as Stanfield, pride might make him dig out the cash. But did he have it? If not, wouldn't he want to show how much his neon reputation meant worldwide by getting the first consignment on account?

Becky felt him stirring and reached under the duvet to take hold. 'Yum, yum,' she said.

'True,' he replied.

She slid down in the bed, nimbly despite everything, and put her lips against the end of his cock. That was the way she always did it, never making it easy by taking it in an open mouth. She liked him to push her lips open and her teeth, as if she was reluctant or even against, not welcoming. He did not mind, it could improve things. This was some happy seduction fantasy of hers and she was entitled to it. They read all sorts of stuff these days, and women's satisfaction discussed on Channel 4. All the same, he never went mad in her mouth, that deep-throat carry-on, because it could be dangerous and selfish, especially with someone prettily pregnant. Never would he come during oral. That was uncivil.

'You taste lovely,' she said. 'Not just of you and me.'

'Of the future,' he replied.

She came up the bed again and he climbed on to her gently. Stuff Stanfield, you might say. He went into her gently, too. But after that, the gentleness had to go. She did not seem to mind. She looked happy. With skill and passion you could always fuck worry out of a girl's face for a while.

When he was dressing, she said: 'Going out this late, be careful, darling. Get a good look at the street from the window first.'

She was telling him his trade, but all right. This was only her caring. 'Now, *my* instructions to *you*, love. Lock up when I've gone and don't open until you hear my voice,' he replied. 'Nothing to worry about, believe me, but not until you hear my voice.'

'Is this Stan Stanfield you're meeting?' she asked.

'Stanfield? No. He's told me all he knows about France.'

'It is him, is it, Keith? You're seeing him for something else now.'

'I told you, Stanfield is France and only France. France is still a possibility for us, obviously.'

She turned on to her side to watch him. 'Well, I still want to go,' she said. 'It really would be wise, Keith.'

He heard something too definite in her voice. 'Hey, have you been trying on your own – seeing Harpur, something like that?'

She did not answer at once, but then said: 'Keith, darling, I told him I would go alone. Didn't want to, but would.'

'Told Harpur that? Jesus.' He was sitting on the floor, pulling his trainers on. He stopped and stared at her. It hurt to realize Harpur knew this damn girl would ditch him. That would bring some heavy police laughs. They loved people to be left high and dry. They could pick them off better then.

'It's all right,' she replied. 'I can't. He says no money.

You're the only one they worry about. It's regulations, in Magna Carta.'

He knew this would be some bit of learning, but he did not ask. Why should he crawl? Sometimes she would do that, shutting him out. He felt a real hate for her come up, and even for the baby. Women, they had no solidity, no regard for what was right and decent. All they considered was survival. 'You would have gone without me, Becky?' He pulled the second shoe on and stood up. 'What, secretly? Secretly, like you went to see Harpur?'

'I thought you would come after me then. After me and the baby. It's my last shot, Keith.'

'But you would have gone alone? Doesn't anything mean anything to you, for Christ's sake?' He waved at the bed and the flat.

Becky lay back and shut her eyes. 'Harpur said no money for me, but I wonder. I wouldn't trust him.'

'Who trusts police?'

'Would he tell me if there was money?'

'Why not?' He knew she would have an answer. She was all brain and belly.

'Are you bait, Keith? I stay, you stay.'

'Bait? How?' He wanted to get out of here, leave this painful, amateur talk, find Stanfield.

'They must still want those three who got off. Iles won't forgive something like that, will he, lie down to some judge? Are they waiting for them to come after you? Harpur and his lot could get on the scene then and knock them over in the street or here, and it would be very legal and very neat.'

'Total shit,' he replied. 'They wouldn't be allowed. That's savage. Not even Iles.'

'Who wouldn't allow it?'

'Their boss, of course.'

'Would he know?'

'This is a police force. Every bugger knows everything about everybody.' What she said scared him. Harpur, Iles, they could probably shut out that tender, frail sod at the top whenever they wanted. Those two together could manage anything. They could get Saddam. 'I must go, Becky,' he said. 'This is an important little get-together. Money in it.'

'Money?'

'Not immediate. Long term – the best sort.'

She kept her eyes shut. 'Don't get ratty now, but look, I thought about that money you had the other day. The new maternity dress? This was right after that post office was done and the Pakistani dead.'

He had his hand on the doorknob, but stopped and turned. 'Post office? Listen, Becky, if I—'

'This is a day-killing in a busy street. But the police get nowhere.'

'Who said?'

'No arrests.'

'It could have been a smart job. There might have been real preparation.'

'Do you think they're going easy? Don't want whoever did it inside yet?'

'Crazy,' he replied. 'You don't have a bloody clue how police operate. If they had anything they'd jump. All they think about is their score.'

'Iles and Harpur might think it's a bigger score to see off Beyonton and the others. Never mind who gets hit with them.'

'Crazy,' he said again, leaving. She failed to see some jobs might be done so well that not even Harpur would get anywhere.

Keith was twenty minutes late, but Stanfield had not arrived. Either that or he had turned hoity-toity over the wait and gone. Keith thought he would give it half an hour, although he hated this spot. When the moon came out now and then from under the clouds, all you saw was the old concrete observation post and great stretches of flat, fat mud. It shone brown and black, with occasionally a great wedge of grey-white effluent dancing across it, hustled by the wind and breaking up into fragments, and then these breaking up again. It was like dreams in a fever. The sea was somewhere, just about audible as the tide picked its way back up towards the shore. Nature. It needed help.

At a quarter to midnight Stanfield arrived with Beau Derek. When the moon got to him, Stanfield did not look as smug as usual. 'Sorry, Keith. I thought I had a tail. Took a while to lose him.'

'You mean you *did* have a tail.'

'It's possible.'

Vine stared back to where they had left the cars. 'You're sure you lost him?'

'Would I have come and involved you if I hadn't?'

Mr Considerate. 'Who'd tail you? Police?'

'Could be.'

'Why?'

'You know what they're like. They get an idea. It will go away.'

'Or to do with screwing Jack Lamb's girl, Stan? He knows a lot of rough people. He can be rough himself. You safe in a remote spot like this?'

'No approaches *re* the post office?' Stanfield replied.

'Christ, a tail. I mean, Stan.'

'It happens to all of us now and then. Our name comes up on the computer for a spell of harassment, like time for a teeth check-up. Anyone of any significance. Never happened to you, Keith? Means nothing. I like it out here.' He took a good, long, worshipping look towards the glossy filth. 'It's not pretty-pretty.'

'Fucking haggard, I'd say,' Keith replied.

'Stan and I hate anything showy, picturesque,' Beau said. 'The nitty-gritty's what grabs us.'

They called Beau Derek that because his name was Derek and there was a star, Bo Derek. It was a joke, and some would say Derek was, too. He was nearly bald, short, with a face he got by with, but only just. But he could do safes.

'Couldn't you give up this girl for a while, until we get things really going, Stan?' Keith asked. 'Have someone else pro tem?'

'What do you think of this lad, Beau?' Stanfield replied, like a hiss. 'The things he says?' They stood outside the defence post. 'But Beau and I still think it could work, the three of us.'

'We ought to get going fast,' Keith replied. 'There's all sorts of minor boys cutting themselves little slices of Kenward's business. Some could start thinking bigger.'

'Like Alby and Josh,' Stanfield said.

'Kenward spent years building that organization and we don't want it splintered now,' Keith replied.

'Stan and I can see the possibilities, but it's got to be admitted we don't know the drugs trade,' Beau said in his respectful little voice.

'Of course you don't,' Keith replied. 'I know what you're good at, brilliant. I can soon tell you how this business goes. But what I needed, need, was someone with stature, someone to give cred. Doesn't matter which kind of business it comes from. So, Stan.'

'Stature? You mean money?' Stanfield said. This was him as big, straight-out Stan.

'That could come into it,' Keith replied.

'What are we talking about?' Stanfield replied.

Keith said: 'I heard forty grand was nice to start with. You can get enough stuff for a real presence on the streets, and the pushers know you're going to be around for keeps – not just someone lucky with a bit to supply this week but not next.'

Beau said: 'We spend forty, get what back?'

'Beau's the figures man,' Stanfield said. 'Why we need him.'

Yes? It was true, though. Beau was feeble about everything but safes and counting. Give him a lock, give him

125

some sums, he was not recognizable. 'Yes, we do need him,' Keith replied. 'At least double, and maybe even a hundred grand. But say just eighty. Stan and you get half your forty investment back, leaving sixty. We put all that in the next purchase. This is mostly coke, maybe some Ecstasy. We take no profit for ourselves from the first couple of consignments, until we've paid off that up-front money and got the business really running. So, we turn sixty grand into a hundred and twenty at least. You get the second repayment, which leaves a hundred to buy with. The hundred we turn into two, and maybe at this stage we take ten grand each directors' fees, leaving one hundred and seventy grand for doubling. These are all low-expectation figures, but it's best to do it like that, no disappointments, no extravagance.' Let dear Beau know he was not the only one with a calculator. But Jesus, what a spot to chat finance.

Stan was leaning pretty relaxed against the blockhouse wall. That could mean either they had forty grand and did not need to worry, or that they did not have forty grand but wanted to look as if they did have forty grand and did not need to worry.

'The tale around was you had a few bloody good takes which you didn't throw about, Stan,' Keith said. 'One yarn was you even did Kenward's own safe just before he died and got something untold.'

'Beau's the boy who looks after all that side, the capital side,' Stan replied.

'We could go to forty,' Beau said.

'You wouldn't be putting in anything yourself?' Stan asked Keith. But no wait for an answer. 'These post office jobs never really produce,' he said. 'Too much sodding money going out, not enough coming in. It's the welfare state.'

'As I see it, I bring the trade knowledge and the con-tacts,' Keith replied. 'You're the bankers. You back my flair.'

'Flair's lovely and very crucial but bankers want a bit

more returned than they put in, Keith,' Beau said with a deeply friendly laugh. 'We risk forty we should see fifty back. Say on the first dividend Stan and I take fifteen each, you ten. That's if the period is not too long. What time are we talking about between each deal?'

'A month,' Vine said.

'So we've got twenty out for one month and another twenty for two,' Beau replied. 'Yes, I'd say ten grand fees would be reasonable – not generous, but all right. We're partners, after all. We won't want to screw one another, I hope.'

'That post office,' Stanfield said. 'Why is Harpur sitting on it?'

'What's that mean?' Keith replied.

'I'd say they're not rushing,' Stanfield said. 'They're letting someone run free. Why?'

'Who cares? Nothing to do with us, is it?' Keith replied.

'I hope not,' Stanfield said.

'How quick?' Beau asked.

'What?' Keith said.

'When do we need the forty?'

'Right away. I can go to a supplier with a smile on my face then.'

'They'll do us credit eventually?' Beau asked.

'Maybe fifty per cent,' Keith replied. 'Especially if they know it's Stan.'

'I've got no name in drugs,' Stanfield replied, going so humble. Maybe the mud stench had dazed him.

'Not in drugs, but in general,' Keith said. 'They realize they're dealing with someone who knows business practice, not fly-by-night, someone with weight.'

Beau said: 'Well, maybe they'll do credit from the start.'

'Nobody's got that sort of name,' Keith replied. 'They wouldn't do first-deal credit for the Pope. Nor second. Maybe third. Us maybe third, too, if they see we're getting ahead. The bigger our operation, the bigger theirs. They'll help us along. They've got outlook.'

'Right then, done,' Stanfield said. He took one more

127

long gaze at the mud flats, stocking his soul with memories for when he was back in town. He moved off and Beau tagged after.

'For God's sake keep an eye for Jack Lamb,' Keith called, but neither of them looked back. This would be another case of someone giving it to a girl just for the pleasure, no real thought about the significance or the future or even the dangers. It was so casual and sixties.

Keith had a great giggle about them on the way home. He loved the pomp. *We could go to forty*, says Beau. Vine also loved all that crude, sneering cheek – Stanfield asking if Keith would be putting anything in himself; knowing he wouldn't and couldn't, and going sniffy at the post office job. Some would turn mad at this treatment, but luckily Keith was too big and balanced for that, big enough to pity them and get a laugh. The main thing, the only thing, was Keith had turned out right again, and these two could do the finance. Chief mark of a great leader was he could spot talent and cash.

He parked two streets away. This was a vandal risk, obviously, but it could be a bigger risk to appear as a nice sitting target in front of the flat. He did a little roundabout tour on foot and came in through the lane entrance. All this pissed him off. He hated skulking again instead of taking charge. He had been feeling so good about the deal with Stanfield, but now he had to sneak about around his own place because of some offal like Beyonton. He stopped for a couple of moments in the little rear yard, making sure everything looked right. They would know about back lanes, too. He glanced up at the window of the flat. It was dark, intact. Of course.

And then the thought came to him suddenly, like a thump in the gut, that it was all too still and serene and dark. The reaction was stupid, he half knew that. What else should the place be but still and serene and dark? But it persisted. It persisted because of what Becky had said earlier about leaving alone. Christ, what if she had taken the chance to desert, police money or not? Some of her words had made her sound so desperate, as if ready to write him off. He had half noticed it at the time and her words rolled over him again now – the hard way she read the situation, her evil guesses, her smart guesses, about him reseeing Stanfield, about the post office, and the bits about bait and a police ambush. Maybe it had all finally sickened her, made her run, not willing to be tied to someone so dumb any longer. The idea paralysed him for a moment, took his senses. Although he was still gazing about the yard, he saw nothing.

He edged out, key in hand, towards the rear outer door and the stairs to their flat. A notion he had shelved after Stanfield's warning about the need for tranquillity suddenly returned. He must get rid of Claud. That was positive, and it would achieve so much so fast. If she was still here now – she must be, must be . . . if she was still here, Becky would feel more at ease about staying once Claud had been removed. This would also certainly take out competitors because, even if Foster and Gerry Reid tried to go on, Panicking Ralphy would want immediate exit once he knew the syndicate brought peril. Panicking must be their main lad now, he would not come in as less. If he went, that was the end.

He let himself in. It was not the sort of building where you had a light on the stairs and he paused again, listening. Everyone knew about stairs – they turned you into the most lovely target. But his fears of a trap were less than the dread that Becky had gone. God, please let her be there. He tapped the flat door and quietly called her name. Almost at once he heard the bolt drawn and chain undone. 'Hello, darling,' she said, 'what time is it?' She looked so magnificent – burly, smiling, fair hair a nice rough mess, her face soothed by sleep.

'I've got to nip out again, love,' he replied. 'Go back to bed. I won't be long.'

He went to his hiding-place among paint pots in the

utility room and brought out the holstered automatic. Despite the hazards, he had not taken it earlier, afraid Stan would notice as before and start rewondering whether Keith was too much gung-ho trouble for partnership. He fitted the holster and put his jacket back on before returning to Becky.

'What's happened?' she said.

'I want you to be happy and comfortable, love.'

'I would be if you came to bed.'

'Long term,' he replied. They just could not think like that.

Chapter 20

Yes, Harpur had always thought some women were at their most beautiful and desirable during pregnancy. At three or four months they took on a lovely composure and their skin seemed to grow finer, almost glistening. In the radiant patience of their faces you could read happy, safe continuance of the human race. Becky was like this, probably more than any woman he had ever seen, even Megan. Christ, Becky was wasted on that sad little jumped-up nothing, Vine. Would Keith know how to reverence her and what she told of? 'This is a wonderful surprise again, Becky,' he said. 'Everyone.'

Returning at about 2 a.m. after a night with Denise, Harpur found his daughters up wearing dressing gowns, and Becky in her antique-shop maternity gown seated on the living room settee. Iles wearing a leather jacket, jeans and brown Doc Marten boots was perched on a corner of what Harpur still thought of as Megan's desk. They were all drinking cocoa. This sort of thing did happen now and then when Harpur returned from late outings: one or other or both his daughters downstairs and the ACC present. The visits of Becky were something new. Harpur could see that Iles was inspired by her in this state, too, and he gazed at Becky and sipped the cocoa caressingly, as if his lips were already in touch with some worthwhile part of her.

Jill said: 'Becky's here again because her man's gone. Now. In the middle of the night. She's terrified for him,

Dad. She came looking for you again. We couldn't get hold of you anywhere, naturally. So Hazel said to ring Mr Iles. Well, she would.'

'I explained you were out of reach on a surveillance matter, Colin,' Iles said. 'Regrettably, duty means we can't all sleep at home every night.'

'Martyrdom suits him, luckily,' Hazel replied.

'Your control room said they couldn't reach you, Dad,' Jill said.

'Radio silence on this kind of work,' the ACC told the girls. 'The sound might disturb the target.'

Hazel coughed a bit, often a sign she was going to say something brutal. 'Dad, you don't actually go into the student residences and – well, and stay, do you? Have you thought you could be recognized, a big old object like you among youth, and that butcher's shop haircut?'

Yes, he'd thought.

'You'd be better of with her here,' Hazel said.

Yes, he'd thought of that too, but so far, Denise would not do that when the children were at home. 'Gone where, Becky?' Harpur replied.

'She thinks he's in awful danger, Dad,' Jill said. 'Not just general, like before, but at this moment. Oh, look, her man called Keith came home in the middle of the night and then went straight out again to somewhere extremely secret. I mean, this is too much stress when she's going to have a baby. But you know his name's Keith, anyway, don't you, one of your failed finks?'

'Please, find him,' Becky said. 'I do realize you've probably got your own interests, both of you, but please find him.'

'What's that mean, "interests"?' Jill asked.

' "Interests"?' Hazel said. 'Interests in a business?'

'Some upset between you and Keith, Becky?' Iles replied. 'This seems to me like your typical young couple's quarrel.'

'No, no, it doesn't,' Hazel shouted. 'Mr Iles, you're

putting on a show. Dad, please: what's behind it all? What are you trying to stage? You two.'

'But why in danger?' Harpur asked.

'Do you know what you sound to me, Dad – you sound like guilty,' Hazel said. 'You're playing some game.'

' "Stage", "game" – what is this, Hazel?' Iles asked.

Jill went into the kitchen to make Harpur some cocoa. He sat down alongside Becky, Iles and Hazel opposite.

'Find him?' Harpur said. 'But where do we start?'

'I hoped you'd know,' Becky replied.

'She hoped you'd know because I think she's got a good idea where but can't grass on him although he's a grass,' Hazel said. 'She wants your help. Why don't you move? Move! But you don't want to, do you? To me it looks – it looks as if you just won't interfere with whatever it is. Some police plan. I know it is.'

'He came home and went out again?' Harpur replied. 'Where had he been first time?'

Becky did not answer. Jill returned with the cocoa and sat down on the floor, her head against Harpur's legs. Sometimes, she liked to give him a bit of shielding from Hazel. Both girls were anti-police, but Hazel was older and so more committed. 'Did Keith have a piece, Becky?' Jill asked.

'Stop talking like San Francisco police on telly,' Harpur said.

'Is this some, well, vendetta after that court thing?' Hazel asked.

'He could walk into a trap?' Jill said.

'Are you carrying something, Dad? Iles?' Hazel asked.

'Of course we're not,' Harpur replied. 'This is a British police force.'

'Yes,' Hazel replied.

'Please,' Becky said. 'Find him.'

Harpur loathed the intensity, the devotion. Did she know this lad killed?

Iles said: 'We'll take Becky back, Colin and I. My feeling, he'll be at home now. Lovers' tiffs are always so grand to make up.' The ACC's face twitched minutely and his voice trembled. He might have bone-pain to think of her making it up with Keith.

'We'll come,' Hazel replied.

'You must go to bed,' Harpur said. 'It's a school-day tomorrow. Today.'

'We'd better come, Dad,' Hazel replied. 'We could be useful.'

'How?' Harpur said.

'I shouldn't think Becky wants to be alone with you two.'

'Oh, thanks,' Iles said.

Hazel and Jill went upstairs to dress. 'Was he armed, Becky?' Iles asked.

She did not answer.

'If so, we ought to draw a couple of weapons ourselves,' Iles said. 'In case he provokes something in others. In case he's outgunned. We could help him then.'

'You've been waiting for this, haven't you?' Becky answered, her voice down to an angry whisper. 'Anyway, you're so bloody slow, it will be over. You don't care who gets shot as long as it's someone. Reduces competition, regardless.'

'Was he armed, love?' Iles said.

She did not reply.

They drove over in Iles's car to Keith's and Becky's flat, Harpur in the passenger seat.

'Which is yours?' Harpur asked.

'I bet you know, Dad,' Jill said.

'Where the lights are on?' Harpur asked.

'Yes.'

'Did you leave them on?' Harpur asked.

'He's back,' she said.

'We should come in with you,' Harpur replied.

'No,' Becky said.

134

'Becky, they ought to,' Hazel said. 'They're not much good at trials or detection but quite useful on the heavy side, especially Iles.'

'The detective is dead,' Iles said. 'Trials are for paying lawyers.'

'No, they can't come in,' Becky replied.

'She doesn't want to be seen with cops, I expect,' Hazel said. 'Who does?'

'She came for cops when she thought trouble,' Jill replied.

'People are like that, Jill,' Iles said. 'They get ambivalent when needy.'

'Yes, but he might go mad if she arrives with police,' Hazel replied.

'I thought he liked police,' Jill said. 'He informs for them.'

Hazel said: 'I'll go in with you, Becky. In case.'

'No,' Iles replied.

Harpur had been going to object, also, but then decided it would almost certainly be Vine there alone. Harpur disliked echoing Iles on many things, but especially the welfare of his daughters.

Hazel said: 'Tell him you went out looking for him, anxious, and you bumped into me, a stranger, who calmed you down and brought you home.'

'What are you supposed to be, a girl of fifteen walking the streets alone at half past two in the morning?' Iles replied.

'You know all about that,' Hazel said.

'It might not be Keith up there,' Iles replied.

'Who else?' Hazel asked.

Iles said: 'Intruders.'

'What intruders?' Hazel asked.

'Any,' Iles said.

'I think you know which, don't you, Mr Iles?' Hazel asked. 'Some scheme.' She left the car quickly. 'Right, Becky?'

'No,' Iles said. 'I'll come.'

'You can't,' Becky replied. She climbed out of the car after Hazel and they walked towards the front door, Hazel half supporting her.

'No, you can't, sir,' Harpur said.

'This is your daughter, for God's sake, Harpur,' Iles replied.

'They'll probably be all right. Who else would come back to his place if – if there's been trouble?'

'What's that mean, Dad?' Jill asked.

'If there's been trouble,' Harpur replied.

'If he's been killed? He's gone hunting and got hunted?' Jill asked.

'Damned casual, damned cool, Harpur,' Iles said.

Hazel returned after about ten minutes and got into the back of the car. 'OK,' she said. 'What a puffed-up creep.'

'Did he look all right?' Harpur replied.

'A creep. "One had urgent business, late as it might be. So grateful to you, little lady." '

'A sweet reunion?' Jill asked.

'I think there will be,' Hazel said.

Iles sighed. Harpur saw he was driving back to Arthur Street via Claud Beyonton's district. The girls noticed, too. 'You *did* know where he went?' Jill asked.

Iles slowed as they passed Beyonton's semi. It looked dark and at peace and they went on. They could not call and check he was all right. How would they explain their worry? It would look like harassment and you did not harass the acquitted. Worry? Who cared whether Claud was all right, anyway, except for keeping score?

'Shall I tell you how I see it?' Hazel said.

'Well, no,' Jill replied. 'Maybe they don't want to hear. All sorts of things don't get talked about but they're there. These two are like that.'

'There's a war and you're trying to stir it,' Hazel said. 'Becky's in the middle. You couldn't care less about her.'

'That's absurd, Hazel,' Iles replied. He would have

come in when they reached Harpur's house, but he said he wanted to sleep. 'Dad's had a tiring time,' Hazel told Iles. 'The surveillance you mentioned, Mr Iles?' Harpur could not face an endless analysis of the night from the ACC, nor questions about why Keith was not being watched, nor accounts of his instant veneration of Becky and details of his bracing plans for her.

But Iles appeared in Harpur's office first thing next morning, brimming with all these things, alight with praise for Hazel's sharpness. 'My impression is, she and Jill might warm-heartedly but misguidedly subsidize the girl to get out, in the absence of official funds. Would they have money, Col?'

'A bit of savings, I expect. Hazel keeps a sort of escape fund.'

'Whose escape?'

'Hers.'

'Well, we don't want her to go, and we don't want Becky to, either. I mean that mainly from an operational point of view, of course.' While Iles was itemizing Becky's capable hips and articulate breasts, the Chief knocked and edged around the door chummily on his beige socks. The ACC said: 'Here's the Chief himself as it happens, now, Col. Fortunate. We were discussing Vine and his woman. Rebecca something, yes, Col?'

'Sounds rightish.'

'A wan little object, sir,' Iles said. 'Nice, but hardly a girl to get one's gristle tightening, not even Harpur's, and he's easily moved, as you know. We've talked to both of them, together and separately and at length, about leaving. We, of course, mentioned your kindly personal offer to see them, and to recommend finance for each or both. They're grateful, sir, no question, and would not have you feel anything personal in their rejection. But at this stage they think they must stay. Bonds, pride – not to appear "runners", as they call it. I think I'm putting this fairly, aren't I, Harpur?'

'They're aware of the hazards,' Harpur replied.

137

'My God, this is appalling,' Lane said. He spoke at Harpur's notice-board. 'And then, well, these rumours.'

'Which would those be, sir?' Iles asked.

'Terrible, absurd,' the Chief said. 'A journalist friend of our press lad, Bob Tarr, is badgering him about a supposed incident at the Monty the other night,' Lane replied. 'To be blunt, McCallion's widow accusing you and Colin of partnership with Beyonton and the rest.'

'As you say, sir, absurd anyone could suspect Col of that. I'm going to call on Mrs McCallion, poor thing,' Iles replied. 'She's no treat to look at, but deserves condolences.'

Lane said: 'Well, Desmond, I'm not sure—'

'I feel I owe her that,' Iles replied.

'But to be drinking with those people in such a place,' Lane said. 'That is true?'

'I've got them much in mind, sir, don't fret,' Iles replied. 'I'm looking for an opening to get all three of the sods.'

'Desmond, these are free men, against whom we have nothing.'

'Exactly why Harpur and I thought a drink with them would be a happy gesture, sir.'

Chapter 21

It was not fear that made Becky run. And it was not disgust at the way Keith's life seemed to be going, was going. She rarely went in for disgust. Yet the way Keith's life seemed to be going, was going, meant her life had to go the same way unless she did something. Yes, of course, you expected that in a partnership, but lately she knew she had been reduced, made nearly powerless. Christ, she would not take that. She had an education, could probably have had an executive career if she had bothered. Running showed she could still choose what she wanted, act as she wanted, even without police money. They would not tether her here, Keith and the police in their different, self-serving styles. She had to do it now, before she grew too heavy and awkward, and before she had a pram to push.

She packed a holdall and the new, smart leather rucksack Keith had bought her. This morning, he was out again on something. He had the gun with him, the Russian automatic she was not supposed to know about. The other day she had lifted it from behind the paint pots, taken the pistol out of the holster and held it flat on her palm. She could see it had a kind of neatness, and there was a nice weight and balance. Keith would be excited by all that, and the Russian name. He might want it only for defence. Oh, yes, he might. But that late-night outing had not seemed like defence. It might only be to build his character. Oh, yes, it might. This morning she had not

139

asked where he was going and for what. He would have given her an answer, but she would know it was a lie. He lied because he was Keith, but also to be sensitive, not wanting her troubled now. Off and on, he could be so delicate.

Becky hated all this adoration of her belly and daft tenderness for her state of mind. Although she loved the feel of the child inside, and was sure she would love it when it arrived, worship of the grim, week-on-week process and her stretched shape she could do without. She was not regarded as herself. Men looking at her and wanting her were not thinking of Rebecca Day. They were after a link-up with hope, fertility, survival of the species. Keith was like that. Those two police were. Sex experts who said men lost desire for pregnant women must use a poor sample. These three – Keith, Harpur, Iles – and many others, thought their wandering cocks picked up sanctity if occasionally in touch with the long human story, and especially its forthcoming instalments. Running, she was Rebecca Day again, not posterity.

She would put the rucksack on her back and carry the holdall. Her raincoat should hide her lump pretty well. She thought pregnant women hitchhiking looked idiotic, like a sixties road movie on small-hours TV. She had a little money, enough to take her a long way, if used carefully.

She still thought about France. For her it kept its aura of happy escape, anonymity, new beginnings. She had comfortable pictures in her head from books and post-cards – of course, the red tiles, then wide, easy-paced rivers lapping pretty towns, and grey castles stuck on hillocks with a white sun behind their turrets. More than anything, it was the shitty way Keith corrupted the France idea that made her feel fooled and hemmed in. He told her he went to Stanfield for tips on life over there, but she knew – absolutely knew – that these meetings were about staying. They were behind Keith's new, sweep-the-

140

board career hopes and smart visions. Anyone could smell it. What she had longed for, and he had pretended to long for, he was twisting to what he wanted. Pick a crook, you got crookedness, but he should keep it for work.

She took a bus towards the motorway link. She would get to London first, then a cross-Channel port. As a matter of fact, some of her money could be regarded as police money even now. Those two daughters of the cop had told her they wanted to help although their father and his bosses refused, or especially because they refused. Hazel said she always kept a fund for emergencies. They put their savings together and came up with nearly forty pounds. Becky told them it must be a loan, and she meant it, but the girls said a present to the baby. This was great of them, just kids themselves, and a cop's kids, yet it had angered her, it was typical. They would back a baby who did not exist and failed to see it was she, Rebecca Day, who needed the support, who deserved it as herself, not as Eternal Mother and Nine-month Canister. The girls would give it to her baby, their father would give it to her man. What about Becky? The rest of her money came from her own savings put away when Keith scattered some in good times, or taken now and then from his clothes, just tens and fives, to be unmissed. Choose a crook, you gave him some crookedness.

The bus put her down and there was a ten-minute walk to the link road. She felt pretty good, strong and sure she was right. She had not packed very much, so the luggage was manageable. In her head the notion of France remained wonderfully intact. It meant break-out, independence, the right to decide. Over there alone she might be able to get fruit-picking for some weeks, while she could still manage it. That had a nice peasant touch, the tough yet still presentable woman under a straw hat working in the fields despite her state. Perhaps it would not be necessary. As soon as she was settled, she would write to Keith and he might come, loaded with police

141

loot. She thought he *would* come. He genuinely cared for her and the child. She never doubted this. He certainly cared for the child. But the decision had to be forced on him, and by acting as herself she would help. Just now, he was addled by those status dreams and possibly some dark little successes. Getting the meetings with an eminence like Stanfield would be a triumph on its own, but she knew there had been more. She must drag him out from all these horribly fragile, dangerous schemes. In the end, he would be grateful.

Reaching the link road, she took off the haversack and stood alongside it and the holdall. She did not thumb, but the picture said it all. But, my God, hitchhiking! She was a girl again, exploring the country at about Hazel's age. It was safe-ish then, as long as you could talk your way around trouble. Perhaps she should not blame those two kids for the way they saw things. They would be brought up like all girls in such homes to think sweet thoughts about babies and always put them first. In fact, Becky had not minded the Harpur household too much. Generally, she felt stifled in one of those steady family places, and knew why she wanted Keith. But Harpur's home life was not so steady. He seemed to go his own way, and the girls did too, and would do that more as they grew up. Just the same, he was the police. You couldn't get steadier than that. And all those bloody heavy, mostly old, books around the walls! They shouted, Here we are, here we stay, we're past, present, future.

Of course, most drivers were wary of a woman, apparently alone, looking for a lift. They were scared they might pull in and then her boyfriend with Walkman, camp gear and pit bull would emerge from the bushes. She stood well clear of bushes and did all she could to seem solitary. But the first vehicle to take any notice of her and stop was Keith's Escort.

'Oh, Becky, love,' he said. 'Not necessary at all.'

'Yes.'

He did not get out of the car or open the door, but leaned across and spoke to her through the lowered passenger's window. She was not sure what that meant. Did it say he would let her go, not interfere? Did it say he knew her will would collapse and she would climb into the car with him after a chat? Because of the angle he was at, she could see the butt of the pistol in its homemade shoulder holster under his jacket. That did not offend her. She had picked her kind of life, and guns might be part of it. What depressed her was that the automatic had been bought only lately, and it was bought to make things safer for them here. Why? Because he was staying and assumed that if he stayed so did she.

'A mate saw you walking and called me on the car phone. You're noticeable, Becky, even without the luggage.'

'Thank him.'

'I did. I don't want you hitchhiking, love. Alone, my God.'

Traffic sped past them. In a minute, a police patrol was going to see or hear about the discussion on the link and come to find what the trouble was. If she could spot the gun, so might they. If a patrol knew she was on the road, Harpur would soon. And Harpur was certainly part of the rotten conspiracy to hold her here. They would fence her in and crack her determination. They wanted to use her. They wanted to use her first in the usual way, if she could judge by Iles's face behind the cocoa, and Harpur not much tamer. Above all, though, they wanted to use her as part of some secret, soiled police move, which she thought she could guess at. Well, she was trying to give two fingers to all of them, including Keith. She had thought she was away.

'I'm going to write to you as soon as I get there, Keith, love,' she said. 'You ought to move off now.'

'No. As long as I stay, nobody's going to pick you up. You're mine.' He gave her the smile she knew had been constructed long ago to look wry and masterful, and now it was. She could not work out how to deal with it.

'Please,' she said, and shifted a little back up the link. He reversed until he was alongside her again.

'They'll think we're arguing terms,' he said.

'Twenty people will have taken your number, in case it's trouble. They could report it on their phones.'

'Best get in,' he replied. 'I'll drive you to the next exit. You can start from there. On the way we'll talk.' He pushed the passenger door open now and shifted back behind the wheel. Looking at the open door and the car interior, she felt that same sense of imprisonment hit her again. But so did the same sense of wanting to be with him as ever, never mind his tricks and big-chinned, crafty smiles. And she could tell him to make a better job of hiding the artillery. They still belonged to each other. She threw her bags into the back and took the passenger seat.

'I'm trusting you,' she said. 'I have to get to France, Keith.' It came out not bold but weak, like a petition. She closed the door. They drove on to the motorway.

'I was expecting it,' he said. 'Well, that kid you brought back to the flat, or the kid who brought *you* back to the flat the other night – that was no kid off the street, obviously. You'd been somewhere. Harpur's again? What is this, a second home suddenly? A cop has adopted you? This was Harpur's kid, doing his dirty work?'

'Someone who wanted to help.'

'Harpur's kid? He has a daughter? You're letting him influence you?'

'Harpur's not going to tell me to hitchhike, is he? He wants me here.'

'You'd be chucking a great future, Becky,' Keith replied. He took a hand from the wheel for a second and touched the bit of jacket covering his gun. 'Problems have begun to disappear. Also, we've got capital.'

'I *am* chucking it,' she said.

'No. I can't allow.' He did not glance at her, made out

he was concentrating on the traffic. 'It's not just you, is it? There's the babe.'

'To hell with the babe. Look, pull in now, will you?'

He drove off at the next exit, up and around the round-about and back on the other side. 'You're the most important, but we're a unit,' Keith said. 'You shouldn't talk like that.'

'Why? Who says what I should or shouldn't?'

'Because you don't mean it.'

'We could be a unit, as you call it, in France.'

'We could, and we still can, maybe, when it's time.'

'But it'll only be time if you fail here. And what's fail mean? You're dead? I'm dead? They don't want more corpses in France. They've got the Unknown Soldier.'

'I can look after you and myself. I told you. I'm remov-ing obstacles.' He took his hand off the wheel again and she thought he would treat himself to another fix from the pistol, but this time he touched her arm briefly. 'The lad who saw you walking, he made the point I'm making, Becky. That, if a woman wants to leave, this is her definite right, but when the woman is taking something that belongs to both it changes things. I can tell you I felt right pissed off, having some ordinary lad spelling this out on a car phone that could be broadcasting who knows where like Prince Charles and his lady, as if I couldn't see it all for myself. I'm moving into notable, very hard circles and this lad is telling me and possibly the world I don't know how to run my own home life. You humiliated me there, Becky. He kept barking this word "unforgivable", but I said nothing was that if two people loved each other enough and really wanted to make a go of things. They'll all see it's fine now.'

They were back at their motorway exit, and he drove to the flat.

Chapter 22

Francis Garland said: 'Sir, I've found a couple of witnesses who give me a description of the post office killer that sounds very like Keith Vine, our grass on Alby and Josh.'

'Yes?' Harpur replied.

'But then there's this tip around, picked up by the media, that it was someone who looked entirely different. Bigger. I assumed from you, Col. Your purposes, I guessed.'

'I saw that in the papers,' Harpur replied.

Garland waited a moment, in case anything else came: 'So, am I in deep water?'

'You know what identifications are, Francis. People seeing the same thing see different things.'

Garland said: 'Then a report yesterday from a couple of worried drivers that an Escort registered to Vine is stopped on the motorway link, with a man and woman talking, maybe squabbling, the man in the car, the woman outside with luggage. He's described as like Vine. Not sure about the woman, but his girl? This was a rendezvous? When a patrol gets there they've gone. Our boys assumed they've sorted themselves out and are along the motorway to London, so no further problem. They know Vine's a tricky item since the trial and don't press. Have the pair moved out at last? We've persuaded him? But can we let him go if he did the sub-postmaster?'

'I saw that report about the link,' Harpur replied.

'Why I mentioned deep water, sir.' Garland usually had

146

a brisk, pushy voice to suit his general self, but today he sounded lost.

'What's it mean, "deep water", Francis?' Harpur said.

'Tactics.'

'Mr Iles is interested in it, yes.'

'Some hit-back scheme – for the trial? Is this to draw in Claud and so on, get them in our sights?'

'I shouldn't think Vine and the girl were going anywhere,' Harpur replied. 'More likely he would stop her, take her home. Have we tried their flat?'

'Why say that, Col? I thought she couldn't get money to go alone.'

'She might have landed a subsidy.'

'Where?'

'Society for the Protection of Unborn Babies? There are many generous little hearts about, Francis.'

'Little?' They were in Harpur's office. Iles joined them without knocking the door. He was wearing uniform for some function later. The smooth dark blue of its high-grade cloth, and the muted flecks of insignia in even darker blue and black, always seemed to set off better than any civilian outfit his desperate solitariness and spite.

'Francis thinks it could be Vine for the post office, sir,' Harpur said. 'New witnesses.'

'Really?' Iles replied, and gave Garland a heartfelt beam. 'Well, this is brilliant.'

'Thank you, sir,' Garland said, watching him. 'The Chief's very eager to get an early arrest. He'd hate it to seem we dragged our feet because the victim's Pakistani.'

'The Chief's outlook is not just international, its effects are global,' Iles said. He sat down under Harpur's busy Breaking and Entering chart. 'When he was sick the universe waned and comets dropped short. We'd better not rush at Vine, though, had we, Francis?'

'Hadn't we, sir?' he replied.

'You've been smart to hold back. Typically smart, if I may say,' Iles told him.

Garland, who was standing alongside Harpur's desk, also sat down now, as if aware he'd need all his strength to deal with Iles. Garland was a whizz-kid Chief Inspector, astonishingly brassy and clever, even clever enough to realize Iles was cleverer, when unfeverish.

'You have this wonderful, head-on approach to things, Francis. The way, say, Churchill could chop through the bullshit and get at the essence.'

Garland had begun to frown with concentration.

'It's an aristocratic flair and true gift, Francis, often crucial in our work and, of course, most attractive to women.'

Harpur stood at once and went to close the door properly. He was just in time.

Iles began to shout, pointing an elegant finger at Garland. 'It would be this kind of foul, assertive single-mindedness, this taste for the straight up and down and no thought for others, that led you to screw my wife for as long as it suited you, wouldn't it, Garland?'

Harpur said: 'And you will have seen the Traffic account of Vine on the motorway link yesterday, sir.'

'Exactly,' Iles replied at normal voice. 'Clearly, this is the point.'

'Which point, sir?' Harpur asked.

Garland said: 'My reading of their meeting is—'

'I know as a certainty my wife now regrets that episode, those episodes with you, Garland, and indeed finds them incomprehensible,' Iles yelled. 'And the same as regards Harpur. More so. This was a woman looking for something mentally undemanding and merely fleshly, absolutely and totally merely. You're both tailor-made.'

'Francis thought they possibly rendezvoused there and ultimately left together, sir,' Harpur replied.

'Don't be hard on him, Col,' Iles said conversationally. 'It's not a totally inane view of the matter. If your brain is in your balls, like Garland, thought processes have a debilitating, uphill trek.' He leaned forward, as if a confiding grandfather, towards Garland. 'Now listen,

148

Francis, we've got a sharp one here, Vine. Cool. Thrusting. He's defying us, because he knows he's strong. He hangs about despite lavish offers to set him up elsewhere and actually compels his woman to stay also, drags her out of the as it were departure lounge, afraid that if she leaves he might feel obliged to follow. That's what was happening on the link road. Does this sound like someone who wants to flee our patch because he's done a murder? Does he appear to be afraid of us, of discovery? Can you imagine what the defence would do with that if we charged Vine? Poor old Col in the witness box again made to look an even slower slob than he actually is. Note how he's ageing.'

Garland said: 'Yes, sir, but—'

'I don't know whether you've seen this woman at all, Francis, but she'd have to walk part way to the link and with her looks would cause notice and messages all round. I don't say she's perfect. Both Harpur and I think she leaves a lot to be desired and we desire it. Harpur would have shrivelled right up, I mean more so, if Becky had gone.'

'We'd better check they really are back home,' Harpur replied. 'Francis could be right.'

'I love an open mind.' Still crouched towards Garland, Iles said with a comradely lilt: 'What's so great about your post office insights, Francis, is that they tie Keith Vine undeniably to firearms. Harpur could probably have done that earlier for us, anyway, through one of his other informants. He could have, but he didn't, in that eternally micro-minded, secretive style of his. Keithy's been down to see Leyton Harbinger at The Hobart, has he, Col?'

'That the big pub on a corner, sir, with the parrot?' Harpur replied.

'You see the beauty of this, do you, Garland?' Iles asked. 'Of your splendid work?'

Under his crew cut, Garland's neat face remained untypically blank.

'The ACC means that if Keith has a gun record we're

entitled to carry something when we're watching him,' Harpur said. 'For self-protection.'

'Watching him?' Garland asked. 'I could arrest him.'

'This is what I've been saying to you, rat-dropping,' Iles replied. 'The present case against him is weak and he knows it. This is despite your undoubted, fine achievements, Francis. He'll tough it out, bluff it out. As we're aware, identification evidence is very shaky and confessions useless these days. The detective is dead. We need much more. We'll have to keep an eye for a while. Build something.'

'He's bait, is he?' Garland replied.

'Well, certainly a potential target by enemies,' Harpur said.

Iles reached forward and joyously thumped Garland's arm with his fist, as though a wonderful and totally new thought had reached him. 'What's just occurred to me is this, Francis: if people were to come looking for him because he grassed on the Alby and Josh killers, we'd be in a grand position to deal with that, too, being armed. This would be simply by fortunate accident.'

'You've schemed it, have you, sir?' Garland replied. 'Yes, he's bait. That's why you won't have him pulled in?'

The ACC said: 'In the normal course, if, say, we were to knock over Claud Beyonton, or Harry or Gerry Reid or all of them, please, please, God, though I'd settle for Claud – and we might have to settle for Claud – if we were to knock them over when they were stalking Keithy, a court is sure to ask how come we had armed police present, right on the spot. It could look distressingly like a trap, a plotted ambush. That's what big policing is now, but we don't broadcast. You know what the judiciary's like about guns on the street, especially police guns, and especially when the deads are such undiluted shit as Claud and the other two. Three villain bodies on a pavement, or festooning Keithy's settee, would excite humane comment, no question. Press, Civil Liberties, the Liberal

Democrats, bishops would all launch their wholesome bleats. The Chief might get soulful, too. But if we can say – and we can – we can, thanks to your grand discoveries, Francis – if we can say that our people happened to be there armed because we had surveillance on a suspected murderer who uses guns, we're in the comparatively clear.'

'There could be more than three hurt,' Garland said.

'One of our boys? It's possible,' Iles replied. 'If you do gun training, you ask for the extra risk.'

'I meant Keith. Maybe the woman,' Garland replied.

With a sharp, small groan, Iles said: 'I'd hate to see Becky injured, that sweet skin. Odd, her breasts and so on are what one prizes, obviously, and yet when I imagine her with damage it's the lovely oblong of her back I see cruelly torn and bleeding. Oh, God.' He had gone a bad colour, suddenly. The grief was real and fanciful. 'Ricochets. The true value of your work, Francis, is that it enables me to skirt Harpur, you see. I told him an age ago to put people on Vine for protection. He thought it too dangerous, because our lads could not be armed. Now you've given us the breakthrough. It's this kind of outstanding work that means I'll be eager to urge your promotion, in due course. The fact you were screwing my wife for weeks if not months a while back cannot detract from these other accomplishments, I hope.'

'Thank you, sir,' Garland said.

'Can it, Harpur?' Iles asked.

'I'd still be worried about putting people near Vine and in the firing line,' Harpur replied. 'We've nobody who could handle it.'

'Certainly,' Iles said. 'Listen to the bugger, Francis, flaunting his rare leadership qualities – pious care for the troops. But it's wasted. Simply, this is the sort of job we'd need to handle ourselves, personally. You'll say, inappropriate work for an Assistant Chief, and I'd recognize that. But I'd recognize Claud, too, and this is more important. I've kept up my gun ticket, you know.' Iles stood and made a revolver of his hand, like a boy playing cowboys, then placed the finger muzzle against his temple. 'Pow, pow, pow,' he said. He sat back content and stretched out his lean legs.

Garland said: 'No court would swallow we were tooled up and on the spot by accident.' Suddenly he was almost back to the old assurance, his voice doing its usual metallic bang. Iles used to say if Garland were ever thrown out of the force he could become a steel band.

The ACC straightened, then bent forward again in wholly amiable style towards Garland. 'No, maybe we wouldn't get away with the tale. Our famed British legal system is deftly rigorous and exhaustive in its pursuit of truth, so when it comes to the worst, and it usually does, we obviously say Fuck the courts, as a cosy change from the courts fucking us. Claud dead is Claud dead. No court could take him, or them, off the scoreboard.'

There was a nice little knock on the door and Mark Lane entered gently, also in uniform, including shoes. He and Iles must be parading somewhere together later on. In uniform Lane generally looked as if he had had a series of very bad stomach-upset nights while wearing it.

'Here's the Chief now,' Iles cried thankfully, the parched raft survivor glimpsing a sail.

'I heard voices,' Lane replied. 'I heard Francis. I wondered if there had been something on the post office.'

'Francis is doing remarkably, sir, but nothing of any substance for the moment,' Iles replied.

'It's so important,' the Chief said. 'These minorities. We must be seen to protect their interests.'

'Francis is known around the building as P. D. Garland, standing for Positive Discrimination, sir,' Iles replied. He eye-signalled Garland to get off his chair and offer it to Lane. The Chief sat down.

'This odd report from the motorway link,' Lane said. 'Have they gone, Vine and his woman? If they have, is it without our help?'

'Francis has looked into it and believes just some sort of lovers' tiff,' Iles replied. 'He thinks they'll be home again now.'

Lane shook his head in bafflement. 'Could we check, and use it as an opportunity to ask them once more to go, with our aid, either together or the girl first?'

'Ah, how remarkable, lads,' Iles said, smiling with happy amazement around at Garland and Harpur. 'You're somehow able to intuit the gist of our little meetings, sir. Harpur was just forcibly suggesting that very thing.'

Chapter 23

Keith said: 'I want to show you something, Becky. It proves we're all right.'

He stood up and almost skipped from the room, suddenly so full of himself. She heard what she expected to hear, the paint pots shifted gently, and in a minute he came back, one hand behind his back, grinning with pride. 'Guess,' he said.

'Tickets for France?' She could risk it.

The grin dropped and he went evil-looking for a moment, that big, Sherman tank chin barging forward. Then he forced himself to turn sweet again. The grin edged back. 'This makes tickets for France not necessary, Beck,' he whispered. It was as though they were children with a marvellous secret between them, almost a piece of magic. She remembered when such kid enthusiasms in Keith thrilled her. Less now. The kiddishness put his life and hers on offer.

He brought the holstered Makarov slowly into view, the way a man might with an engagement ring. 'That canvas!' she said. 'My old haversack.'

'Why I bought you the leather one.' He pulled the pistol out and put it on the coffee table. 'Lo!' he said. 'Russian.'

'It looks . . . well, lethal.'

He had a grand laugh. 'Yes, the word.'

'Has it been used?'

'Never, never,' he blurted.

'I don't mean here. By the KGB, or the siege of Stalingrad.'

'Never,' he said. 'That's the beauty. It's not so old.'

She bent and gazed closely at the Makarov. Days ago she had hatched some girlish comment in case he showed off the automatic to her. 'Oh, look, the Russian star on the butt.'

'Eight rounds and good up to fifty metres. Would I carry a used gun? Crazy.'

'You carry it?'

'Now and then,' he said. 'Or why a holster?'

'When?'

'We've got some hazards, Becky. I'd never say we didn't. I can't go unprotected. This puts us right.' He picked up the pistol and handed it to her. 'Smell. That will tell you it's unused.'

After that link road farce yesterday he had stayed with her in the flat for the rest of the day and overnight. He seemed to think she wanted this. Around lunchtime today he went out for newspapers, but only briefly, and she saw he was afraid to leave her long. He was nurse, he was jailer. Now, she took the gun and held it pointing to the ground. Then she raised it slowly and aimed at a picture of some woman in a blue turban that came with the flat. She would play along. It was a habit. It was partnership. She put the pistol back on the table.

Watching her, Keith thought this gun was helpful. Becky would see he was mature and thoughtful now, and would also see how well he planned. She would know a gun like this could not be picked up by just anyone, anywhere. This would tell her he had important contacts dealing in high-quality items. This pistol and the confed. with Stanley Stanfield were bound to bring her a new notion of things. Never would she want to run again. Please, Becky.

He said: 'France? I know you love that idea, feel a true, well, like *amour* for it, yes, and you're entitled. I love it myself, believe me, San Trope etcetera. But what's happened is, I go to Stanfield for pointers and he advises me France is no good at all, or would he be back here? OK, so you ask why didn't I tell you straight off? Well, knowing you'd be disappointed, and I thought, maybe he was just bitter for the moment over something private there, and he would change after a while, which was why I saw him so often. But no.'

'No good how?'

'All ways. Everything tied up between – well, what you'd expect, between Frogs. Obviously, I'm arguing with him full out, but he always says it's better here, the potential, and Becky, love, he's talking like he sees golden promise in me, although youngish, and also though I made this mistake of wanting France. This is Stanley Stanfield himself, not a sidekick like Beau Derek. These are huge prospects.'

'What *he* calls a mistake.'

While they talked she wandered around the living room, and he began to feel jumpy. 'Come and sit down, Beck, love,' he said, 'and I'll explain.'

'I can't relax, can I? It's a twitch. I have to look from the windows all the time, to see who might be in the street waiting for you, or getting ready to come in for us.'

He badly wanted to go and check, in case she had it right. So often she did have things right. He sat still, though, trying to be casual, gazing at a paper. She was beginning to affect him too much, too often, and he must stop it. She took his strength away and he would want all his power and balance soon. But he did need her too, he knew that. Yesterday, he had decided that somehow he had to keep her with him or he was useless. Stanfield would notice, and farewell partnership and the stake. Keeping Becky here did not mean terrorizing her, or not too much, anyway, or locking her up. For Christ's sake, was he like that? Never. No, he must tell her more about how business was going, and how the good future would shape, let her into things more. Well, like today – explaining some of it, showing the gun. She would be almost another partner. He must hold on to her, but not let her force him down.

He said: 'I told Stanfield you were sold on France, naturally, and especially for the baby, and he says it's no place to bring up a kid because they'll go like Jerry any day now and turn against foreigners, torching. The French hate us, we bashed the franc, and Waterloo.'

'It would be different for us there. We'd be given a property. Things would be smoothed.'

'I couldn't tell him because it would say a grassing pay-off, but even so I think he'd be against.'

Keith saw she did not believe any of it, the smart-arse bitch, but he had to go on strong or a whole, brilliant business chance was lost, including forty grand's cash backing from Stanfield and Beau. Christ, in cash! When would you get two favourables like this together again – money ready here, Kenward's empire ready there? For forty grand you could forgive Stanfield anything, the king-of-the-castle walk, the famed palette ancestor, the moustache.

Yet, although he had a career to snatch, he also longed to please Becky. It had hurt him the way she tried to quit yesterday. He hated to think of her suffering so much she could not stay. Her determination always troubled him, that and her bits of education. He knew he was as smart as anyone, but no education, so why was she with him? And yesterday she nearly wasn't. The leather rucksack made it worse, because she'd take something quality he'd bought her and use it to ditch him. Probably she had lifted some of his money for that, too. This was real will.

She was still at the window and he thought he could join her now, without it looking like he jumped when she spoke. He went over and stood close, his arm around her shoulders. He remained shielded by the curtain and took a long, very careful stare, all directions. 'Nothing at all,'

157

he said. 'Of course nothing at all.' He returned to the sofa.

'Nothing at all *now*,' she replied. 'But you did a real squint. You know it's possible all the time, don't you?'

'Of course I came. You seemed anxious, love. I had to comfort you. I knew there'd be no one.'

'Because they're too damn pro to be seen.'

'I think Beyonton's out of town anyway,' he replied.

She began to shout. 'How can you know that? You just say what will soothe me.'

'No. Come and sit down. I'll tell you how. That's part of it.' He wanted her to take a place on the sofa with him, but she went to a straight-backed chair opposite, keeping alert. This separateness upset him, made him angry. Well, what he was going to tell her was pretty factual, so she did not need to sniff for lies.

He nodded towards the Makarov. 'That's for defence, absolutely, forced upon me Beck, but what's defence? This is the point. I decided I don't wait here, peeping from windows like Neighbourhood Watch, scared Beyonton and the others will call. Sod it, I thought: Keith, *you* call on *him*, get him out of the way. It's the kind of man I am, I think you know, Becky, not meaning to crow. If necessary, I'll look for trouble, to stop trouble looking for me.'

She put out a hand and gripped the curtain, like she needed support. 'You mean you've killed Claud Beyonton?' she asked in a weak whisper. 'But you said it hadn't been fired.'

He loved that amazement in her voice, and the adoration. Although they came a bit too soon, he was entitled. He had known all this would change how she saw him. He knew she would want to stay now, because he could prove he'd see off all her little worries. 'No, he's away,' he replied. 'I've been to his house a couple of times these last few days and nights with my Russian friend – broke in looking to wipe out the mouse bastard, but he's not there. He will be, though, one day soon and then we—'

'To shoot him?'

'You know this word, pre-emptive, Beck? Well, of course you do, your background.'

'Why's he away? He knows you're coming?'

'Could be that. He'd realize Keith Vine is not some victim.'

'He'll see you broke in. He'll be ready.'

'When I say broke in, I don't mean anything was broken. What am I, some boy burglar? He won't find signs. I looked around in there for him, that was all, took nothing, disturbed nothing. Taking from him would be – I don't know – cheap?'

'You went into his house? Alone? My God, Keith.'

He watched her straighten on that chair, so astonished and nearly not believing, yet believing. She knew Keith Vine was capable. 'It seemed to me the simplest thing,' he said. 'It's while I'm sitting in the car near his place, waiting, I get the call about you. Why it upset me so much, Becky. I'm out at business, trying to make our prospects healthy and ordered, and then I hear my girl's doing a bunk, putting herself on a plate for drivers.'

'No takers,' Becky replied. 'Only you.'

'I have to be with you,' he said, and there was a genuine small, helpless sob with the words.

Still at the window, Becky found it all a bit touching. She saw that yesterday really had changed him, a little. Yet to her everything seemed totally and hopelessly the same: the dangers, Keith's vanity and greed and weakness and obsessions. She had been freighted back here from the link road, and Becky could not really blame him. Oh, he had promised he would free her at the next exit, but she knew it was a lie, and realized getting into the car was surrender. As ever, someone had to do the thinking, someone had to show sense: Becky. Police might have arrived at that display on the link and begun asking questions, possibly seen the gun. The gun that killed a postie?

He said no, it had not been fired. Perhaps. In any case, she did not know this yesterday. Keith could be careless. He was reading the *Daily Express* now, but looked up and gazed at her occasionally, his face hard and expectant, big-chinned again, waiting for her to crawl for forgiveness. She said nothing. She should apologize for stopping his mad, hallowed crusade to blow a hole in Beyonton?

He said: 'Jesus, Beck, here's a judge's son in the paper, a *judge's* son, kicked out of his top public school for theft and drugs. I mean, what right to lord it, telling us this and that and putting people away, if they get such kids? It's always happening. Do the buggers deserve friends like me?'

'They don't listen to friends like you,' Becky replied. 'So, which judge?'

'What? Does it matter? It's typical, that's all. A judge, a full wig.'

'I wondered, the one from your case – the one who let Claud and the others go?'

He went back to the name. 'How the hell did you know?'

She cringed to see him awed by a bit of ordinary sense, as if she was a witch. 'It figures. The police would want to kick him in the crutch. If they can't nail him for pederasty, fix his children.'

He wrinkled his face. 'Police knock a judge? Jesus.'

'This boy Iles, he doesn't let go, does he?' she replied.

'What, you mean Iles framed a school kid?'

'Created it somehow. Especially the press cover. That's what will damage dear Daddy, get the giggles and tut-tuts going at the Garrick club.'

Keith began to laugh. 'Christ, though, that Iles!'

'Yes, that Iles,' Becky replied.

'What?'

She yearned for Keith to work it out for himself, or he might feel stupid again. You had to pump up his sad ego. Did he see that if Iles hunted the judge he would hunt

Claud and the others, too? And the safest way to hunt was not to be seen hunting them but to wait until they came hunting Keith, certain that they *would* come. This would be another of those 'Armed police!' shouts, just a bit too late. She and the baby and Keith could be in the thick of it.

His good, square face flickered for a moment, and she saw he understood. Then he leaned over and touched the gun. His pretty answer. He would reach Claud first. She had wanted him to think of Beyonton as a menace again, get scared and agree to go, and instead he fondled his eight-round toy to prove they'd better stay. He could be such a fool. So, she had tried to leave. But he could also be such a lover, in his style. As soon as they got back yesterday afternoon from the motorway, they had to go to bed, of course. This was supposed to show he still really prized her despite the run. Mainly it was just possession: he had lost something, he had it back. He was saying, I'll have you because you are mine, but he was also saying, Please have me, because I'm yours, and I'm hopeless alone. She could respond, and did. It was better than a shouting-match on the motorway link. She had sensed he wanted to tell her things held back till now, bind her to him by opening his secrets. And so she expected it when he revealed that cure-all pistol. She still saw nothing that dealt with her fiercest wish: to flee this area together now, fast and safely, while they could. Oh, God, she thought, will I ever understand him and his sort? Occasionally today she had heard a terrible, suspicious anger crackle behind his standard boasts and self-pity.

Now, he suddenly asked: 'I mean, where did the money come from?'

'What money?'

'If you're going to France there's got to be money.'

'I had some saved.'

'Saved so you could go? You've been secretly getting ready? How long, for Christ's sake?'

'In case we both went.'

'If we both went you wouldn't need savings. There'd be police money. Or did you have police money anyway? Harpur fixed you up? He's been looking after you, that cosy way he has? I'm not one to search a girl's handbag, as I'm sure you know, but he's been helping you along?'

'No police money. Keith, they made it very clear only you qualified for funds. You were the principal figure, me secondary.'

That pleased him, as she had hoped it would, had known it would. It fitted his view. 'Yes, well I was their star. It didn't come off, but I was still their star. I'm personally owed.'

'Definitely.'

Offhandedly, he said: 'If you want money, come to me.' He gave a snarl-laugh. 'I don't mean for running, obviously. But normally. There's plenty.'

'Good.'

'You want to ask where from, don't you, Beck, but now you're a bit scared? You think I'm ratty.'

'Where from?' she asked.

The anger seemed to go from him. 'A gun like that has to be paid for,' he replied. 'And don't think I can't afford a new holster, just I like making things.'

'It's great.'

'That's our tomorrow and next week and next year and next millenium, Becky love,' he replied, pointing to the Makarov. 'That in the hand of Keith Vine. I know you're grateful, deep down.'

Chapter 24

The four were in a big-engined Rover, Gerry Reid driving today. They had a tanked up, G-reg Granada 2.9 waiting as switch vehicle on a nice piece of hedged-off waste ground about three miles from the bank, mainly through backstreets, tough for pursuit, as long as Gerry was as good as they said. With Ember, all these plans were standard thinking, almost an instinct. He had wondered about a second switch but decided one would do, also as long as Gerry was as good as they said. You had to have faith, even when working with someone like Claud. The vehicles were fine, powerful models, sharp on manœuvring, plenty of room for plump cash sacks.

With any luck, there should not be anything behind them. He did not believe luck favoured the brave, as some said, but believed it often favoured him, and this was obviously better. He had chosen the exit route and found the waste ground. Foster and Gerry Reid picked up the right cars. On some points those two and Claud were very adequate, as Ember admitted from the start: low-rank, low-skill points, like car theft. Discipline, strategy, leadership they had to send out for, and he provided, gladly. They would have loved to send out for easy money, also. That was not on offer from Ember, but he would show them how to find it, lend them his past. He had skipped a lot of university lectures for this operation, so it had better work. He would have to do private reading on the Huns for his history module.

They were about five miles from the bank and the action. You would expect people to be tensed up, focused on the problems, maybe final-checking the armament, but Claud in the back with Harry Foster still snarled on about what he found yesterday at his house. Or what he said he found. Reid drove today because Claud wanted to be 'on the pavement for the hit', as he called it in his big, bad-lad language. He and Foster swore Reid would be great behind the wheel, and it kept Gerry fairly quiet. This time it was Claud who did the talking.

Of course, he should never have gone to his house, anyway. Ember's orders were the four of them stayed sealed off together at Gerry Reid's for two days and nights, building team knowledge and full trust, rehearsing all the drills, preparing for unexpecteds, like astronauts. The only outings should have been Reid and Foster for these job cars yesterday, as late as possible to reduce search time, as if police ever searched for stolen cars. Then they discover Claud's been back to check his place is all right, not invaded. Who's he expecting, Huns? His story is, he spotted possible observation on the house one day when Ember took them to view the bank. No cer-tainty, just half a vague idea, but it made him forget the rules, or ignore them. Ignore them, the arrogant sod. Discipline? Bright, bloody Claud thought discipline was for bondage freaks. He had come back yesterday scream-ing he knew as fact somebody had been in the house since he left, and they heard about it over and over at Reid's flat and now, in the car, on their way to the cash van and whatever came.

'I tell you it's Vine,' Claud said. 'Nothing taken or even moved, gorgeous break-in technique. I spotted the signs, yes, naturally, but few would. So what's he doing? He's not searching, he's not thieving. Obvious – he's looking for me. This was a kill mission.'

'Yes, you told us,' Ember said. 'Lucky I moved you out. You could be dead in your nightie.'

'That nobody prick comes stalking Claud Beyonton like the SAS. I'll have him, as soon as this lot's over. We should have done him straight after the trial.'

'Right,' Ember said. 'Get him when it's over. It won't help business, putting police pressure up again, but if you have to, OK. For now, forget it, though. Just think what we've got to do.'

'I know what we've got to do.'

'Great,' Ember said.

Claud said: 'If some rubbish grass decides he can hunt on my property it's because that rubbish grass thinks he's suddenly reborn as something large-scale and prime. Keithy would never try that in the old days. Ralph, he's got to be looking at Kenward's empire. All at once he sees himself as mighty. He's into some alliance? So, putting him out of the way *is* to do with business. See?'

'Christ, leave it, will you?' Ember replied. He was staring ahead. 'We should see the van any time now.' He loved "on my property", as if Claud's semi and crazy-paved backyard was Chatsworth. 'So, somebody might be outside your house, somebody might be inside. Or possibly not. You're haunted?'

'You don't believe it?'

'What I believe is there's work to do.'

'Maybe you get too narrow and fenced in, Ralph,' Claud said. 'Which brings the panics.'

'What panics?' Ember said.

'Here she is,' Reid said.

The van appeared ahead of them again. It came from a different side-street this time, supposed to be security. But always it had to join the main road somewhere near here, and within a time bracket of twenty, twenty-five minutes, which anyone could timetable. Pathetic, really. Reid dropped back. He had seen the drill on rehearsal. But this was the easy stuff. Escape driving was what counted. Ember could not know if Reid had it, and would not know until there was no hope of changing. All sorts of totally brainless louts, even more brainless than Reid, became true artists with a getaway car, and Gerry might be another.

'Pity we can't hit the van, too,' Foster said. 'It's heavy from other calls.'

'We don't do armour-plate, we do a couple of worried, young-middle-aged, unfit family men in the open,' Ember told him, 'and if possible with no damage.' They did not seem to understand: you named your job, you kept it limited and exact, you put your mind on that and only that and you went on thinking how to cope with any rough, surprise matters right up until you had done it and were away. Sweet Claud called it narrow, and with his poky little face he'd know narrow. Ember would say precise. Anyway, he hated all this backchat. It did not panic him, that stupid, cruel word. It unsettled him, though. Was he too old? Jesus, he was doing the job as it should be done, readying himself, yet this pair with their drivel made him feel past it. Even if the raid went right, could he stay long term in partnership with these clowns?

The van pulled in on the same double yellows spot. Ember wanted to see how many guards left. Sometimes it was three, more often two. Two obviously made things look easier. But three might mean a fatter load. If three went to the bank the driver would be included and that must be against instructions, because the van would be unattended. The two were supposed to make more than one trip across the pavement if the quantity was up. You took them on the first, obviously, because who knew if they'd go back for seconds? Two men jumped out now, as the Rover passed. They looked about for a few moments just as the training said, doing steel and vigilance with their faces, and once again Ember in the passenger seat turned to give them the back of his head. He hoped Claud did likewise or the Identifit artist could soon match descriptions by cheesing a trap.

Gerry parked. The other three left the car immediately

and began walking back, together this time, towards the van. Gerry switched off, as instructed. A running engine was a comfort and meant no starting problems and maybe thirty seconds saved, but a running engine also meant smoke from the exhaust, and this could tell a tale when the car was close to cash on the move. Ember took one glance back at the Rover. He felt the usual terror. It was about more than Gerry's driving. The waiting might rip Reid's nerves and make him crack and bolt early, *with* the sodding vehicle, of course. That had never happened to Ember, but it did happen to some. Of course, the driver would be seen to afterwards by comrades and/or relations, but afterwards was afterwards and did not help people stranded. Someone on foot, running with money bags, was conspicuous, and you might not have a hand free for protection with the pistol. Who could run loaded three miles to the Granada?

Ember cut the pace of their walk. Timing had to be perfect. They would mask up for the actual attack, but must not do it too soon or the alarms would start and the guards stay inside and slam the bank doors. Yet you could not leave it too long, either, or you were in monitor-camera range. Though this bank was across the frontier from Harpur and Iles's patch, pictures went everywhere and those two would love to help do Claud and Harry Foster, even if it meant they were locked up and safe from slaughter. Ember knew Harpur and Iles would love to help do him, personally, as well. Police had this contemptible, envious streak for anyone who put a little money by.

The guards appeared in the bank door and had a short pause and another look around. The older man carried two bags, the other, one. You could never guess how much was in them, but they looked hearty, hearty enough to make the guards nervous.

'Pray twenties and fifties,' Claud said.

Fucking brilliant. 'Masks when they move,' Ember

replied. Through the van windscreen he could see the driver with the mike up to his mouth doing continuous commentary. There would be plenty shouting for help once it started, so an extra voice did not matter much. Ember walked a bit quicker now. You had to watch for a dash and the money flung into the van's chute. He was studying the two lads with the cash. They seemed to change most weeks and you never knew what you'd get.

Some people did not like looking too hard at men you might have to hurt or worse. They kept them as a couple of money porters in crash helmets, and the violence stayed impersonal. That was sloppy, not professional. You had to read the opposition, try to guess how they would act. These two were both thinnish, tall and possibly fit. The one carrying two would be around forty, his mate in the late twenties. Generally it was the older guards who gave trouble. Their generation thought bravery was manhood. Dad told them about D-Day. But the older one of these had a gentle face with very small, almost girlish features. He had grown a bit of a moustache to inform the world he was warlike, but it did not work. The youngster had a craggy nose and very thick neck for such a lean body. He might be on weights. He looked too damned strong, and stupid with it. He could give the problems on this one.

The pair began to move towards the van and Ember said, 'Now, then.' They pulled on balaclavas and Claud and he produced the pistols. This was the kind of moment when Ember would sometimes disintegrate, feel his spirit run away and all his hot ambition burn out. Today, though, he was fine. Definitely fine. Foster would not carry a gun, but brought out a piece of piping with a heavy brass nut screwed on one end. They ran hard. There were people between them and the guards, mostly clerky-looking and harmless so far, plus a couple with a child on the man's shoulders. The child saw the masks and laughed. Nobody else did a thing, except look frightened. It was not their fight. Stay that way. Ember still felt good, his legs bouncy, eyes clear, breath easy. He brought a Walther from his pocket. He used to have a Baby Browning, but that had to go a while ago, after use. The Walther was a better stopper, anyway. He had been to Leyton Harbinger at The Hobart to hire for himself and Beyonton. Claud had a big .45 Smith and Wesson 645, was waving it now. They ran in silence, no yelling to scare. If the weapons didn't do it, shouting wouldn't, and noise only told every pedestrian for half a mile what was happening. Some of those could show brave, or get on their mobile phones. More voices. And more voices: the guards had seen them and were talking into their neck mikes. This raid had coverage.

The young guard unhooked his stick and stepped around fast to stand between his partner and the attack according to the manual, so gallant, so frail. His blue eyes lacked fright, the fool. He was still talking steadily into his mouthpiece and Ember thought he heard both guns named by make, so not so stupid. The young guard roared something at them, not words, more like a howl or groan. When he swung the truncheon it was not at anyone's head but a waist-high sweep to get the pistols. No, not stupid at all. He hit Claud on the gun wrist and his 645 went clattering towards the gutter.

'Shoot the sod,' Claud screamed. 'I'm wide open.'

Ember took a two-hand grip on the Walther and pointed it at the young guard's chest. 'Put the sacks down, put the stick down and stand still,' he howled. Jesus, that neck mike. Was he on the air and on record himself, now?

The young guard looked dazed to have done so much. He or the other one could have dived for Claud's weapon on the ground. Maybe it was not in the training. They knew truncheons, not guns. They both went frozen for a second. It was Harry Foster who bent for it and threw the S and W to Claud, and it was Claud still in a fear rage and with his wrist adrift who fired twice from his left hand at the young guard and hit the other once. Only a fraction of him was unshielded by the younger lad, but it was the best fraction and Ember saw where the big bullet smashed his chest and threw up bone and blood and tunic and heard it whine on after exit and bang into the bank masonrý, still keen on destruction. The man fell at once, releasing the sacks. The other turned to him for a second and Foster instantly leapt forward and hit him on the jaw with his cosh, and as he staggered kicked his legs away so he fell on top of his colleague. Claud bent and shoved the muzzle of the 645 into the man's mouth. Claud might have fired again but Ember grabbed his skinny shoulder and shoved him away. Foster leaned over and dragged the guard's helmet half off. Then he hit him heavily twice on the head with his slab of iron, and the guard moaned and seemed to sink lower on the body of the other.

Ember took two sacks, Foster one. Claud could do nothing with his injured hand and needed the other for his pistol. Often in situations like this, Ember seemed to end with the biggest part of the take, just by the way luck liked him, or by grab. So, he'd got rich. But this was all for an investment pot, and did not matter today. They ran. The couple with the child were in a doorway now, and the child had stopped laughing, just gazed as terrified as its parents.

Christ, a furniture van stood where the Rover had been and at once Ember knew Reid must have heard the shooting and gone. He felt an abrupt and hellishly full rush of the panic symptoms, thick clouding of his eyes, a spasm across the shoulders, his scar seeming to bleed like Bosnia, and the sweat of sweats, his back a lake. 'That fucker, Reid,' he gasped. 'Didn't I know it, *know* it?' The Rover pulled in alongside them smoothly as they ran and they piled in with the bags, Claud in front this time. Gerry gave it the accelerator.

'I had to shift, for a delivery. Went round the block,' he said.

'Great lad, Gerry,' Ember said. 'We all knew you'd be fine.'

'God, you reek of sweat, Ralphy,' Foster said.

'At least,' Claud said.

'Went all right?' Gerry asked. He drove beautifully, effortlessly.

'Easy peasy,' Foster replied.

'We've got nothing behind,' Gerry said.

'It's a triumph,' Foster said.

When they transferred to the Granada, Ember thought it time to repair his status. He took the passenger seat again, the admiral's chair. They would just cruise now, then ditch this car too, and go back separately by public transport or taxi. 'I knew the trouble would come from that young bugger.'

'So why didn't you do something?' Claud replied.

Foster was counting. 'Looks like seventy grand plus.'

'Forty into the business, then seven five hundred each for being good boys,' Gerry said.

'Maybe we could do more than forty for investment,' Ember replied.

'You're the boss, Ralphy,' Reid said.

'I'll need a bit to pay off the weapon,' Claud said. 'It's going into the river, not back off hire to The Hobart. No future for it at all. They'll be quizzing every armourer for miles. I'll get something else to do Vine.'

'Come in Smith and Wesson, your number is up,' Foster said.

'Claud, you fired?' Gerry asked.

'He fired,' Ember said.

'Unavoidable,' Foster said.

'Well,' Ember replied.

'Unavoidable,' Foster said.

'Just the wrong bloke,' Ember replied.

'It worked,' Foster said. 'There wasn't a wrong bloke.'

'We're clear, we're in business,' Claud said.

'It's not the gun's future you should worry about,' Ember said. 'Its history, though, maybe.'

That really banged Claud. His squeak went even

171

weaker. 'Christ, Leyton wouldn't let out a used weapon.'

'How would he know?' Ember asked.

'There'd be rounds missing.'

'The hirer would say just practice shots,' Ember replied.

Claud said: 'If Leyton—'

'Think about it, Claud,' Ember replied. 'A lad hires from Leyton. He knocks someone over with the gun. If he doesn't bring it back, Leyton knows it's seen action. He looks in the paper, watches TV news, and ties his gun to the incident as soon as he hears the ballistics. Now, the hirer wouldn't want Leyton and all The Hobart to know what he's been at, would he?'

'So he returns it and says nothing?' Foster asked.

'Right,' Ember said. 'He's not obliged to tell Leyton anything, just pay. Police will look twice as hard if they think someone's done more than one job with the .45.'

'But I bloody haven't,' Claud replied.

'Not how it seems to them,' Ember said.

'You mean I ought to take the Smith and Wesson back, or Leyton knows for sure I killed a guard?' Claud asked.

'I'll be taking the Walther back.'

'But you didn't kill.'

'You fucking killed?' Gerry said.

'The heart,' Ember replied.

'Some shooting,' Gerry said.

'Yes, some shooting,' Ember replied. 'It's a tricky one. Harbinger could guess at it, anyway, if the bullet details reach the media. Guessing is only guessing, though. The point is, Claud, we're going into a rich business. Do we want Leyton where he could whisper in your ear one day?'

'What?' Claud asked.

Ember said: 'Obviously, whisper that he'll take a cut of your profit, or he'll talk into someone else's ear about an unreturned .45.'

'All right,' Claud replied. 'I'll hang on to it for a day or two, think about it.'

'Think hard,' Ember said.

This was what he meant. These three could do the basics, such as driving, hammering, even some sort of shooting. It was the forward planning they fell down on, the intricacies of power. He felt very content he had let them know this. His sweat had finished altogether now, and that terrible feeling in his jaw scar.

Chapter 25

Harpur spent as much time as he could now watching Keith Vine's flat, especially at night. Occasionally, Iles would come with him and once in a while the ACC did a turn alone. They both went armed. For Iles, it was his cherished cleansing trap, entirely that. Harpur understood the thinking; even sympathized, half sympathized. But whose thinking? It was the ACC's, and this would sometimes start from injury and rage and progress to frenzy. Iles and the Chief both feared wholesale evil had begun to triumph, might not be stoppable. Now and then Mark Lane looked ready to surrender or get invalided out for good. Iles, though, glared at the foe from high in his turret of bright malevolence, and still had the strength, hate, vanity and imagination to resist. The ACC said it was his personal duty to hold law and order in trust, with occasional minor aid from Harpur. There was nobody else.

For Harpur, to lurk around Vine's place was protection of Becky, almost entirely that. It might have been protection for Keith Vine, too, but perhaps Keith had wiped out all obligations now. Becky was the real worry, and the responsibility. Harpur's silence about Lane's offer might kill her. The detective is dead, long live the anxious, guilt-sick bodyguard.

In Iles's view two of them could easily take on Beyonton, Gerry Reid and Foster, especially as Harry Foster never did guns. The ACC believed that he, personally, could handle the three alone with his Bulldog Magnum. He was not sure about Harpur. 'Christ, but you're pitiably short of higher management evil, Col,' the ACC had said. 'I want a radio-call at the slightest sign of them, if it's a night when you're solo, Harpur.'

'Bring a contingent, sir.'

'I'm not a contingent but I am who I am, Col. We don't share our targets and *gloire* with the heavy mob, do we?'

Tonight they were in Harpur's car, down the road from Vine's flat. Harpur had a Colt King Cobra .357 in one pocket and his small metal cosh in another. 'There'll be one hell of an inquiry aftermath, sir. This is an Assistant Chief and a Chief Superintendent actually lying in wait, tooled up.'

Iles purred. 'Gorgeous phrase, "lying in wait", like some hungry, graceful animal. Say a panther, or lioness.' He fondled his grey mane. 'Aftermath leave to me, Harpur. My doctorate's in Aftermath. We've discussed all that. These people murdered yet are free because of a palsied system and your incompetence, Col. They can smile, plot, carouse and screw unparalleled pussy like that young Deloraine. This is grievously inequitable, but can be remedied here, fortunately.'

The ACC had functions to attend and a wife to keep happy, so he did not appear every night. When he did, he throbbed with satisfaction as if having finally defined his career purpose: to knock holes in Claud and perhaps Gerry Reid. Possibly even unarmed Foster, in the rush of the moment, especially if that left Deloraine to be repeatedly distracted by him from grief.

'In a way I'm sorry for Beyonton, Col,' the ACC said. 'He's become more than himself, and a challenge. Suddenly, Claud's an emblem of victorious villainy. At my level, Harpur, one learns to spot these big, symbolic moments and to create one's own counters. I must demonstrate now that courts may fail but justice never. And so, to crack the bugger open with two hardly separable left-tit shots becomes an undodgeable mission like – oh, I don't know, say—'

'John the Baptist, sir. I saw you fucked up the judge.'

'There's a daughter as well yet,' Iles replied. They were watching from the car's rear window and he suddenly tensed, as though having spotted something. He pulled the Bulldog from its holster. After a while he relaxed again, though. 'I hear strange tales from our next patch neighbours.'

'About the Smith and Wesson 645 that killed the bank guard?'

'About the Smith and Wesson 645 that killed the bank guard,' Iles replied. 'Thanks, Harpur. Would you ever have told me?'

'It's rumour only, so far. Our colleagues have released nothing official.'

'Of course those bastards release nothing official until they're compelled. They hoard what they have, the way you do. It's called policing. So, Keith Vine twice? From post offices to banks? He's climbing the ladder fast. Well, we certainly can't let the bugger flit to France or wherever now, can we, Harpur?' He sounded delighted.

'The 645 could be hired.'

'What? Bloody what! Leyton would let out a weapon already used in a killing? Remember, Harpur, this is a respected businessman.'

'Leyton might not have known. But he and his lady have disappeared. Perhaps they fear comeback. Perhaps they're already in the sea.'

'The Hobart wouldn't be the same without them, would it?'

'Is that the big pub on a corner, with the parrot, sir?' Harpur replied.

Night after night they saw little to interest them at Vine's flat, but Iles's blood-yearn never faded. 'They'll come, Harpur. Claud's integrity's at stake, and you can't go bigger than that.' Vine went out now and then, but he was not Harpur's priority, and Iles regarded himself as too poor at tailing to stay unseen: the ACC sometimes had startling moments of humility. They would sit together in the car and wait for Vine to return, chatting quietly, or less quietly, about Iles's standard main topics. He was convinced that any attack on Vine would happen here, near or in the flat. Now and then as he watched the ACC toy with his Bulldog, Harpur thought Iles would not really mind being shot to pieces on this kind of task. That would take him fully into the symbolic. He would suffer meaningful death on the job, ridden down by galloping rottenness. Not just a saint, a martyred saint. Harpur recalled his using that finger pistol against his head, as though he could not be bothered any longer: a touch of the Mark Lanes. The detective is dead.

But, no, for Christ's sake. Mad. The ACC must never crumple like Lane. That was catastrophe. In any case, Iles had shaped things too lovingly to want to go out yet as a haloed failure, and especially not crushed by some mouse-faced slice of crud like Claud. The ACC found so much to enjoy, and to continue enjoying. He lived for his wife and daughter, lived for bullying and vandalism, lived for the force, lived for giving it to girls as much under twenty as was humane and even legal, lived for the longer poems of Tennyson.

Iles asked gently: 'Notice how Deloraine looked at me in the Monty? You know the girl I mean? The one with *Comfort Me* tattooed on the white of one eye, eight-eenish.'

'Unique. Those glances were appetite, yet more than appetite – a plea for true, spiritual rapport, also, sir.'

'Ah, you spotted that. Sometimes I think you're not as stupid as everyone says, Harpur.' Iles sighed. 'My life is an eternal search for someone who can see my worth, Col, and I felt Deloraine might.'

'This is a perceptive girl, sir.'

When Iles left tonight and Keith was still out, Harpur

knocked the flat door. She opened up at once, 'Look, Becky,' he said. 'I'm here to say there *is* money after all for you to leave on your own.'

'You knew all along?' she asked. 'Your conscience piping up? Suddenly scared you'll make me into a sacrifice?'

Not suddenly. 'Can you go?' he said.

'When?'

'Now.'

'I'm only just back.'

'Get further than the link road this time.'

'You have the money with you?'

'Some money.'

'Your own?'

'The rest can follow.'

She seemed to consider. 'No,' she said. 'It's too late.'

They were talking on her doorstep. Tonight he could feel an immovable hostility towards him as cop, the kind you often met in young people who deliberately went down a social notch. Not even Iles would get anywhere here. People like Becky behaved as if they thought Harpur would expect someone with her accent and background to side with the police in any true crisis, and so she had to show non-stop and full-out she did not. But Harpur expected hardly anyone to side with the police. He white-knighted alone, or occasionally with Desmond Iles. 'Can I come in for a minute?' he asked. She moved aside and he closed the door after him.

'How too late?' he said. 'You're still alive. I've got a car outside. Keith's away.'

'Too late, because I see the situation.'

'I hope so. If you see it you'll go.'

She made some tea and they sat in the little job-lot living room. She had on her antique-shop dress. As far as he could tell, she did not need maternity clothes yet. Perhaps emphasis on the pregnancy was meant to soften up Vine, make him listen.

'He brought me back,' she said. 'Well, you know.'

'We wouldn't let that happen again.'

She became suddenly intense. Sex boomed. 'But in a way I liked it, Harpur. I liked it a lot. He wanted me as me. That's valuable to a girl. Can you understand?' Her green eyes had lost their usual sleepiness and shone now.

God, women were needy, as needy as poor Des Iles. Harpur felt envious of Vine. He said: 'Of course he wants you. That's why he'll follow when you go.' He realized he had misread her, patronized her. She saw more in Keith than just a racy bit of rough. There was something strong here, and two-way. No, Iles was not in with a hope. Harpur began to feel anxious in case Vine returned. It would be bad to be found alone with her here, and so late.

'Follow?' She nodded and sipped. 'I would have believed he'd come after me. But not now I see the situation. You can't let him go. He's too important to your project.'

'Project?'

'Either you'd stop him coming after me, or you'd bring him back. If I want him I've got to have him here.'

Harpur searched for an answer.

She said: 'Before if he'd said he wanted to go, you'd have accepted it. Your bait scheme would be ruined, but never mind, you'd have honourably seen off your debt to him. And you'd have let him stay abroad or wherever. Now, you can't. There've been some developments, haven't there, Harpur?'

'Which would those be, Becky?'

'You know. So now if he ran and became no good to you as cat's-paw you wouldn't write him off. Couldn't write him off. You'd have to drag him back, do an Interpol, and I lose him for God knows how long. Like for ever.'

He saw she was talking about a dead sub-postmaster. Had Vine said something, or was she sharp enough to guess? Yes. She was also sharp enough not to spell any

179

of it out to a cop. She had just given a damn good esti-mate of how things stood. He would have expected that from her.

'I'm stuck, if I want him,' she said, 'and on balance now, I do. He loves me, depends on me. For myself. It's a sweet, rare feeling, Harpur. Remember? I can't just waddle away. Not again.'

'For Christ's sake get some security on the door,' he replied. 'Stand to the side of it and check who's there before opening. Well to the side of it, as you get bigger.'

Chapter 26

They were at that smelly old defence blockhouse on the foreshore again. Stan Stanfield had a cardboard box under one arm. In the dark, it looked like for a kitchen mixer or something similar, silver and brown pictures of it on the front and back. He put the box on the filthy ground and opened it up. Beau was holding a couple of bicycle lamps, one in each hand, and slowly moved the beams back and forth over the open box, like criss-cross search-lights on clouds. There was a glint of mild colours – greens, browns, blues, and this was it, the forty grand.

Keith felt jubilant. He had a good, loud laugh, because it was such a dirty dump for showing off thick capital. Here was more money than had been in this place for all its half-century. If Hitler had arrived, valiant acts might have been done from this post, but in fact tonight was its finest hour. Thank God he had not bolted to France and missed this grand event.

'So, we're ready to go,' Beau said.

'I see an outfit as big as ICI ahead, and us founder directors,' Keith replied. He would have liked to step across the blockhouse to shake hands with each of them, but Beau was holding the two lamps, and Stanfield might think it a bit showy: he was into aloofness. Keith wished Becky could be here now to view this brilliantly powerful cash. It would make their lives. Above everything he wanted her and the child to be happy and provided for, really provided for. This was the start of that. It was a man's duty. He had another laugh about this drab setting for the birth of a dynasty. When the child was at Eton or Roedean he or she – he did not mind at all, it could be boy or girl – the child would be able to shock them by saying where Daddy's wondrous empire began, alongside mud flats on a mud floor. The child must not be ashamed. Where there's mud there's magic.

He would tell Becky about the money tonight, of course, when he went home, but if only she had been here to look herself as Stan flipped back the cover of that crazy box and you could see the plenty in neat piles! She would have felt all the impact and rich surprise and realized at once how wrong she'd been, trying to leave. He would not hold this desertion against her, though – absolutely no bitterness or rage. She was bright but with a different outlook, and could not be expected to see all ramifications.

'Touch it if you like, Keith,' Stanfield said. He stood away from the box and pretended to stare from an observation slit again, so casual, as if the cash bored him and he always walked about with this much. Naturally, Keith knew what Stan wanted, the holy bastard. Stanfield would love to see Keith crouch over the funds, bend, in worship. This the high-boy would regard as worship of him, not of the funds, and he'd be sure he was entitled.

'I'll believe it's exactly what it looks like,' Keith said and stayed upright. He did give the words plenty of awe, though. And then he thought, *No, Keith, be kindly and humour them, these worthy lads. They've cashed in all their savings-stamps for you.* 'Oh, yes, yes indeed,' he murmured and did get low, knees on the fucking muck, and gently kissed three of the tiny bundles heartfelt, like a welcome to newborn triplets. Beau put one of the beams on Keith's face, so his joy and gratitude could have a nice display. These two deserved this treat, watching him. Forty grand gave people undoubted dignity and Keith decided from now on he had to try to equal this. Well, grovelling here did not look like dignity, but that was just a due gesture. He must concentrate on the partnership, the way they obviously did. For now, yes, this old concrete hut was like their boardroom, and he must behave in tune.

Stan bent down, closed the box and put it close to his feet. Keith stood and brushed the archaeology from his trousers. 'We wanted to show you we do what we say we'll do, Keith,' Stanfield said. He spoke it in a solemn voice, like a marquee preacher. Any moment Stan would ask all who wished to be converted to wait behind. Well, Keith did – converted into someone loaded, so he would stay.

'Didn't I already know you do what you say?' he replied. 'You're famous for that.'

As a first step to his new character, Keith thought he would even forget about Claud. To hunt him the way he did lately was so wrong for a businessman and father, a businessman backed by forty grand cash. It brought stupid risk, that childish, wild tit-for-tat stuff. Christ, breaking into his house was suicidal. And to go back there would be more suicidal, because Claud was smart enough to see someone had called, regardless. Next time, he and friends would be waiting. They wanted him even before this. Keith had to keep healthy and alive or how did he manage the providing, for God's sake, and how could he be a proper partner? Of course, keeping healthy and alive meant he had to deal with Claud if it was Claud who came hunting *him*. That's why he had the Makarov. Everyone was entitled to self-defence. But from now on, only that.

And then, suddenly, Stanfield turned this warm and friendly meeting icy and very perilous. 'We need to know what *you're* going to put in,' he said, a real final-demand voice.

Keith was astonished and for a couple of seconds could not answer. Then he said: 'We've talked about that, haven't we, Stan? I supply the contacts. Where we buy,

183

the good outlet points, street-level pushers. Prices we should pay and charge. All that expert stuff. I know dealers who'll give a true welcome to such lovely funds.'

Beau said in that snivelly little way he had: 'But what about a money stake from you, Keith?' He had switched off one of the lamps and put it down. The other he held pointing to the ground. 'Because I'm Mr Figures, I have to ask. No offence.'

Keith giggled, tried to giggle: 'You know I haven't got this sort of cash. Boys, now come on, I told you from the start. Keithy's no moneybags, regrettably. Yet. That's the basis of this arrangement, Stan, Beau. Surely.'

Stanfield said: 'But maybe there've been changes?'

'What changes?'

Speaking down at the yellow patch of light on the brown floor, Beau said: 'Look, Keith, this is delicate again, but we got some information about that cash van raid in the next manor. The dead guard?'

'The gun,' Stanfield said. 'The word is it's the same as for the postie.' He was still at the observation slit, talking over his shoulder, more casualness, but this could go deep.

Keith had heard about the gun, too. He thought it was great. If the police found someone for the guard, he would be done for the postie as well. True, that could cut the other way. But it was a long time since the post office, and the police were nowhere on it. Of course they were nowhere. There were no leads. They might get the van raider, though. 'So, the same gun for these two outings,' he replied, like fully baffled. 'Does that affect us?'

'Were you on the bank van raid as well, Keith?' Stanfield replied. Some of the light held Vine, but Stan stayed well into the shadows, now a voice in the old third degree.

Keith did a bit of a pause. ' "As well?" You're saying I did the postie?'

'You can see why we'd be interested, Keith,' Beau replied. 'It all comes very close.'

'Christ, this is crazy,' Keith said. 'Two crimes I've hardly even heard of.'

Stanfield turned. 'Well, yes, Beau thought crazy about the van, you not being up to that, Keith.'

In a rush, Beau said: 'Meaning only not up to it *so far*, Keith. No reflection on basic ability, believe me.'

'He thought, post offices, yes, but not Keith Vine for a big cash collection – guards and alarms, all that,' Stanfield said.

'Although you could grow into it, obviously,' Beau said.

'Myself, I'm not so sure, Keith,' Stanfield said. 'My view is you'd be ready now for a big team.'

Keith could have spat at that bald hanger-on, Beau, for this cruelty. All right, it was true he had never done anything as big as a bank van, but this creepy sod thought he could tell just from a look at Keith that it would be too much. Keith liked the way Stan questioned that. Behind the bath-mat moustache he had a helping of brain. 'This is the only big team I'm interested in,' Keith replied. He was glad he had strapped the Makarov on tonight. These two talked like they had been conned by him. Keith shook his head sadly. 'This was a first-class business meeting until a couple of minutes ago, and now such unnecessary aggro.'

Beau was leaning against the wall near the door, his lamp still lighting up his sandals. He looked slouched and half asleep, but that was a pose he always did. He could probably move fast enough to close the exit. Keith tried to read if he was carrying anything. Had he put one lamp down to leave himself a hand free? He had on a track-suit top that was a size too big and could hide plenty. These two had planned their positions.

'Four people on the van job,' Stanfield said.

'Yes, I heard,' Keith replied.

'No word yet who,' Beau said.

'The only word is this gun and the four, all masked, naturally,' Stanfield said.

Beau said: 'Look, Keith, not every syndicate can come up with forty grand, cash, for investment.'

'Don't I know it?' Keith replied. 'Magnificent. You boys are—'

'Possibly the van raid was to supply someone's start stake,' Beau said.

'Yes, I see that,' Keith replied. He gave a small whoop. 'Which lets me out, yes? I'm with you two. Why would I want other money? I've got great bankers, the greatest.'

'But you hadn't seen this cash when the van raid happened,' Stanfield said.

'I didn't need to see it. I had your word, Stan. Stan Stanfield always does what he says.'

'Skip the gush,' Stanfield replied.

'Stan hates compliments, however justified,' Beau said.

'Keith, you're the kind who might like stakes in two companies. You've got your responsibilities now, the girl, a kid. These are dear to you, yes?'

'Sure,' Keith said.

'Sure. To your credit. But this is what I mean,' Stanfield replied. 'You say to yourself, "There's Stan and Beau, they might turn out all right, come up with the necessary, but who's certain? Let's join another team, too, just in case." '

Beau said: 'What Stan means, Keith, is with your sort of career, you're used to being in two outfits at once, or more. You had this police link through the case, but you're also a tradesman – negotiating with us, plus the post office visit and the van. You're everywhere. Some people are born with this jumpiness. They don't feel right, don't feel safe, if they're giving what you could call their loyalties only one way, always expecting to be let down. It's a need they have to be various, Keith. Insurance. They can't help it. But it's bound to cause interest. Your police connection is bound to cause interest, Keith.'

'This is rubbish, a police connection,' Keith shouted.

'The trial and then Harpur's there with you, fancy-dressing in the antique's market, Homburg, buying clothes for your girl,' Stanfield said.

'Look, don't think we've been tailing you, Keith. This was just some information, that's all.'

Stanfield stiffened for a moment and half turned his head towards the observation slit, as if he had heard something outside.

'What, Stan?' Beau whispered.

In a moment, Stanfield relaxed. 'Just the sewage sea, probably, trying to come up for air. Keith, you've heard about this other outfit in the frame?'

'A business team that could also have a police connection,' Beau said.

'God, no, I never knew that,' Keith replied.

'Iles, Harpur,' Beau said.

'What? I don't believe it. They're evil, but not evil that style.'

'You never heard of a rough scene at the Monty? Josh McCallion's widow?' Stanfield asked.

'A scene?' Keith replied.

'Iles, Harpur drinking with Claud and the others. This is full view. In she comes and starts asking how was it the trial collapsed. Some alliance? Why are they socializing, maybe celebrating Claud's freedom? These were very nasty moments for all.'

'That's bloody mad,' Keith said. His right hand was fighting him to get up and touch the Makarov for comfort. He would not let it, though, not until it was unavoidable. Send no early warnings.

'She could be heated, obviously, saying more than made sense,' Beau said. 'But you can see why we're interested in police connections, Keith.' He nodded towards the cash box. 'We put everything on view and we feel entitled to the same.'

'I agree,' Keith shouted again, 'of course I do.'

Beau looked around out into the darkness, as though the noise would bring crowds. They all stood silent for a few seconds.

'I've told you everything,' Keith said, his voice down

now. 'I can't tell you about money if I haven't got any.'

'Let's say Claud, Harry Foster and Reid at this van raid, Keith,' Stanfield replied. Voices did not echo in here, but they sort of clanged in the air, like slamming a metal door.

'I don't see why,' Keith said.

'They've got to find capital fast. They know there's others in the race. The driving sounds like Gerry Reid. So just let's suppose these three, for argument, OK?'

'And then one other,' Beau said.

'What, you're telling me this was Iles or Harpur with them? You can't mean it,' Keith was yelling again. 'On a pavement mission? Never.'

'No, of course not,' Stanfield said. 'That's not how it works, is it, Keith?'

'I don't know. How does it work?'

'They make it easy for people,' Stanfield replied. 'Yes, you know that.'

'How make it easy? This wasn't even on their patch,' Keith said.

'You do know the geography, then?' Stanfield said.

'I read the papers,' Keith replied.

'These boys, Iles, Harpur, they hear so much,' Stanfield said. 'Maybe that the guards would be carrying something unusually heavy on the day. This kind of help.'

Keith was calculating the steps to the door, about six. He would pull out the Makarov as he went and if Beau tried anything he would clobber him with it, or worse. Then out into the night and find cover down alongside the sea wall. In a minute he said: 'I'm supposed to be number four? That what you're saying?'

'It's this 645 that troubles us,' Stanfield replied.

'It does make a puzzler, Keith,' Beau said.

Stanfield went very sad. 'I asked you if you'd supply funds not because we want them or need them, Keith, but so you'd have a chance to say your position has changed. We could understand someone wanting two

188

ways into Kenward's realm. We'd hate it, but we'd understand. Like Beau said, your kind of personality. You say not a thing, though, Keith. You act ignorant.'

'I know Stanley finds this hurtful,' Beau grieved.

'I don't say anything because I haven't got anything to say,' Keith bellowed. 'I don't tell you my position has changed, because it hasn't. I've never been near a bank van raid.' He had already stooped once tonight, so he could do it again: 'Like Beau says – that sort of big over-the-pavement stuff is beyond Keith Vine, so far.' Christ, it hurt.

'That's not the same S and W .45 you're carrying now, is it?' Stanfield replied.

'I'd never use Smith and Wesson. Too traceable. I go for Eastern Bloc,' Keith said.

'Show us,' Stanfield replied. 'But keep the muzzle towards you.' Stanfield just stood there. He did not bring anything out himself, like he knew he could crack Keith just by will. God, the shitty insults. Stan's alleged great-great-great grandfather sketched boats so this prince thought he was immortal.

Beau picked up the other lamp, switched on and shone it at Keith's jacket, over the holster. Keith brought out the Makarov and held it on his palm, the way Stanfield had ordered. It was like showing teacher what you had in your pockets when there'd been thieving.

'That's fine. Put it back,' Stanfield said.

'Oh, thanks very much,' Keith replied. He put it back.

'So why carry it on a meeting with us?' Stanfield asked.

'Oh, Christ, I can't win here, can I?' Keith said.

'Probably not,' Stanfield said.

'You can take that fucking light off me now, Beau,' Keith replied. 'I'm not Shirley Bassey.'

'Sorry,' Beau said. He put the lamp down and still held the other, both on now.

'Why carry it?' Keith said. 'Because I'm hunting Claud Beyonton. Stan, you couldn't get things more wrong. I'm trying to wipe out the sod because of what he did to Alby and Josh, because he's competition, because he's dangerous to me and mine, and you think I'd do a confederation with him. You're a disappointment. I always heard you were good at insights, but now this.'

'Hunting him how?' Stanfield asked.

'I've been into his house at night.'

'So where was he?' Stanfield said.

Beau moved a couple of paces and gazed out from the door. 'We're here too long, Stan,' he said. 'I'm getting nervy. These lights. We're a bit vulnerable.'

Stanfield ignored him.

Keith said: 'Claud was away. But he'll be back and I'll be back. Look, Stan, I can describe the bloody interior for proof if you like.' He laughed again, but not because things were funny. 'I suppose you'd say I was invited there for business meetings, the way your mind goes now.' Get some attack in.

'They could be team-living somewhere before the job,' Beau said. He had gone back to his old position. 'A lot of them do it. For instance, old Panicking often worked like that.'

Beau's warning seemed to get to Stanfield at last. 'Yes, we'll leave very soon,' he said. 'It's almost finished here now.'

Finished? Keith grabbed at Ember's name. 'Panicking? Jesus, yes, Panicking Ralphy.'

'What now, Keith?' Stan asked.

'Number four.'

'Ralph? How come?' Stan said.

'I'm watching Claud's house one day and those three and Panicking come out and drive away in the Saab.'

Stanfield groaned: 'Oh Jesus, Keith. You take your openings, I'll give you that, but Ralphy tied up with Claud? Spotted him at Claud's place, balls. Ember wouldn't look at him.'

Keith felt the whole glorious future sliding away. The

190

Vine dynasty and Eton or Roedean for the child seemed insane visions, now. He might not even survive. He could be the first casualty this blockhouse ever saw. Stanfield had produced no gun when he told Keith to show his, but that did not mean he did not have one. This made the insult even worse. Bloody Stanley had decided he did not need to match the Makarov because Keith was too terrorized to use it. But Stanfield might not leave it to will-power next time.

'Ralphy's another class, Keith,' Beau said. 'Ralphy wouldn't need to do a van for capital.'

'I saw him,' Keith said.

'You say,' Stanfield replied.

'Mind, Stan, it just could be Ralphy's kind of operation,' Beau said. 'Except the shooting. He wouldn't like that. But a van attack.'

'None of this counts, boys – the cars, the team meeting,' Keith said. 'When I see off Claud it will prove I'm not working with him, won't it?' He would have forgotten about Claud for the sake of the partnership, but now he saw he couldn't, not if he wanted to stay in the game and off the slab.

Stanfield said: 'Well, we—'

'So now you'll tell me that could make waves, shake the business.' Keith was shouting again. 'Like I said, can I win here?'

Beau held up a hand and once more glanced back through the door to see if the world was listening. But suddenly Keith realized that this time it was more than just a general call for quiet. Beau remained staring out into the darkness. Then he switched off the lamp in his hand and bent quickly to put out the other. 'Get down,' he whispered.

'What is it?' Keith said.

'Get down,' Beau said. 'Stan, get down and move, for God's sake.'

Keith heard Stanfield shift and went to the floor fast

himself. A second afterwards two shots roared from outside through the observation slit near where Stanfield had been standing. Before he had time to get his face into the mud Keith saw the orange, red spurts of fire as the din erupted and echoed. He heard a bullet crack against the concrete somewhere near him and then the sharp whine of its ricochet and another heavy impact on the concrete. They were caught in a box. Suddenly, the enemy had changed. He lay as still as he could, except for the trembling. He could not draw the Makarov, afraid the sound of movement would bring more fire. He felt like crying out, 'It's Stanfield you want. He's the one shagging your girl. Get rid of him for me.' He stayed quiet, though.

Then he thought this attack might bring chances. Probably, he could get out of here undamaged now. The enemy had changed, but in a minute the enemy might be the same again, Stan and Beau with their sick ideas. Darkness in the blockhouse was thick. He could just see the doorway and the observation holes where the blackness softened a little. Beau was probably still at the door, but his attention would be outside.

Whether Keith made a break or not, he knew he ought to change his position. Whoever had fired might have been watching and listening a while through one of the observation slits, placing them. Still keeping very low, he began to slither in tiny stages across the mud ground. He gave himself long pauses and listened hard each time he stopped. He had to know whether there were people still outside, and he also wanted to know where Stan and Beau were. Jesus, to think he might have been wasting away his time now, bankrolled at some plush wine bar in Cannes, not digging furrows with his nose in the grime of over fifty years.

He found he was automatically moving to his right, away from the door and towards Stanfield. Towards Stanfield and forty grand. He was amazed, yet felt proud of himself for this. He reckoned he had begun to convince

Stan and Beau just before the firing, and might not need to escape. It could be safer in here than dashing loose outside. Jesus, was he going to run from forty grand for something he did not do, when he didn't even run for something he did? Not Keith Vine. In any case, Stanfield might be dead. Someone was after him, and someone very sticky and gifted and who seemed to know this spot pretty well. There was silence in the blockhouse, not even the sound of breathing.

In a couple of minutes, Beau whispered: 'I think I heard someone moving away. Keith, you've got the automatic. Take a look outside.'

They poured shit on him, then asked him to volunteer as target. He did not answer. For all Beau knew, he might be already hit. Now he did edge out the Makarov and swung it about between the observation slits and the door.

'I'll look,' Stanfield replied, and Keith heard him stand nearby and then move towards the exit. Keith could just about make out his shape, but was not sure whether he had the box with him or was holding a weapon. Keith reached out longingly to where he thought the money should be and found it at once. This gave him a real spiritual boost.

Beau lit one of the lamps. Keith was lying with one arm across the box, the other out straight, pointing the gun towards the doorway now. He saw Beau was sitting, unarmed, with his back against the wall, still near the door. It did not seem to trouble him that Keith was cuddling the box, nor how the pistol was looking his way. In a while, Stanfield came back in. 'They got clear.' He had no gun either. He glanced at Keith.

'I thought someone had better cherish this,' he said. He stood, leaving the box on the floor. 'Christ, was this Jack Lamb after you, Stan? Some trigger-man Lamb hired? You're still having Jack's girl? You're tailed this time and last. I thought *I* was the liability.'

Stanfield picked up the box.

Beau said: 'I wonder how much they heard, he heard.'

'We really should leave now,' Stanfield replied. 'Get into some clean clothes.' He came over and picked up the box.

'That's our tomorrows,' Keith said.

Stanfield did not answer.

'Do you want me to do Claud, then?' Keith asked.

He did not get an answer to that, either.

'If I do him, you'll know I'm not his business pal and worth your investment, but will you still be intact to help the partnership, Stan?' Keith asked. Attack, attack. 'Stan, would it be an idea to find a different girl, and let Lamb know? Does it have to be her? Are there unique things she does for you? It's the ballet training?'

Beau said: 'You've got a lot of enemies, Keith, from that grassing. They traced you here.'

'If Keith Vine had a tail Keith Vine would know,' Keith replied.

Chapter 27

Harpur had a call at home from Jack Lamb wanting to fix a meeting. He sounded in a sweat, with something big to say, but not yet. Mostly when Jack came on the line he was triumphal and keen to domineer. Not this evening. 'Peril, Col,' he muttered.

'Who? You?'

'Real peril.' Jack said he did not want either their number one or number three rendezvous spots – the World War Two hillside anti-aircraft gun emplacements or foreshore blockhouse. Lamb rarely talked much on the telephone but seemed to hint there had been dangerous activity at one or other. He was off all military settings. They agreed on a launderette they sometimes used, number four.

Hazel had taken the call. Generally, she would have yelled out something like, 'One of your finks, Dad,' with no hand over the mouthpiece, so Jack on the other end would hear and know what she thought of him. But today Denise was with them in the big living room and Hazel merely signalled to Harpur with her eyes, then handed him the receiver. When he rejoined the girls and Denise, Hazel was outlining a politically correct revision of *Casablanca* where Ingrid Bergman's character ditches both Rick and Victor Laszlo and shacks up with Sam, the black piano player.

'Does Dad talk to you about his trade?' Jill asked Denise. 'This kind of phone session is normal here, the

way other kids' parents get invitations to bridge. That call
– it could be someone's life. Probably. You get a slimy,
worried man's voice asking for "Mr Colin Harpur,
please," but never giving a name himself, themselves.
Well, Dad's told us we don't even ask, and if he's not
here just say "Any message?", which there never is
because they won't give a number to ring back to, and
they're speaking from a booth, anyway. They grunt
"Later", and bang the phone down. If Dad's home, he
takes the receiver like just now and stands there, saying
next to nothing, sucking it all in – like osmosis in Botany
– basics such as "Who?" "You?", getting whatever's
given, or a meeting place and time. Usually after a call
he'll say he has to go out urgently.'

'I won't be long,' Harpur replied.

Hazel said: 'Maybe, Denise, you thought detective work
was clues through a magnifying glass. It's listening to
blabs.' Harpur saw they were initiating her, possibly a
helpful sign. 'And keeping your information secret from
colleagues, especially Des Iles.'

'Do you know him, Denise?' Jill asked.

'Iles is mostly diabolical, and the salvation of the world,'
Hazel told her.

Jill said: 'He fancies Hazel. And almost anything else
under eighteen. Well under. Dad won't take you with him
now to this meeting. Grasses are so super-secret. You can
go home or stay here and wait for him to come back.'

Denise had better recognize this as a critical choice. It
was the first time she had agreed to come to the house
while the children were there. Harpur had done a lot of
persuading. Things had gone passably so far.

'I'd like to stay, if you don't mind,' Denise replied.

She was a talented girl.

Harpur went to the utility room and packed himself a
bag of washing. When he returned, Jill was saying: 'We
can fill you in on much more about Dad if he's not here
spying.' She waved at the shelves. 'Oh, all these books

196

belonged to our mother, not him. His education's a joke. He knows the Bible from childhood and says once he read *Scoop*. We're supposed to be chucking almost all these volumes out, but he just can't do it. Heavy with memories. Should I be saying this to you, Denise?'

When Harpur left he was conscious of the two girls watching, and pretending not to, to see if he kissed Denise. So he did. At the launderette he found Lamb sitting in front of a machine where what could be his army gear rotated. He wore a big-deal outfit today: dark suit smooth enough for Iles, striped shirt, bold tie and narrow, lace-up black shoes.. He looked like a bouncer at a very good club, not the Monty. Harpur loaded a machine and sat with him.

'Hazel sounded quite subdued on the phone. No snarls. She sick, Col?'

Lamb seemed back to composure. 'What's it about, Jack?' Harpur replied.

'Or did you have someone there? Helen tells me you're going to take Denise home. So familial and wholesome. Listen, this idiot boy, Keith, Colin.'

'Which Keith is that?'

'This lad's at hazard.'

'How? And how do you know, Jack?'

'You'd better act, Col.'

'Where does the information come from?'

A couple of youngsters played a chasing game around Harpur and Lamb while their mother unloaded her washing. Lamb joined the pursuit for a couple of circuits, his huge, suave frame hurtling across the little room. He gave Indian war cries. The kids squealed with laughter.

When Jack came back he sat down and said: 'My mother's over with us, you know. She's on at me pretty non-stop about Helen.'

'Doesn't like her?'

'I tried to put things right just the way she'd want, but it didn't work out. There can't be a second go at it.'

'How put things right?'

'Mother thinks everything's so simple.'

'Stanfield?' Harpur asked. 'That still going on? I couldn't help you there.'

'You say. So the upshot is, we're travelling back with her to the States for a while. Mother's suggestion. Make a real break.'

'Helen will go?'

'She'll forget Stanfield and so can I. He's travelled, but he won't come that far.'

'Helen will go?'

'If things had worked out the other night, this wouldn't be necessary.'

'What things, Jack? You tried to get shot of Stanfield?' He corrected. 'Tried to get him out of the picture somehow?'

'Oh, yes, Helen will come. I'm pretty sure.'

'Has she agreed?'

'I'll show her the whole country,' Lamb replied. 'Galleries.'

'She'll enjoy that.' Harpur stirred.

Lamb said: 'Yes, this boy Keith. If I'm gone a while, you'll need someone like him. It's you I'm thinking of, Col. I don't want to leave you without a voice to whisper.'

'This Keith is a source, then?' Harpur asked. 'How does he link with Stanfield and your mother and Helen?'

'He'll try to do Claud Beyonton,' Lamb replied. 'Why I called, basically. To do Claud! You and Iles might say, "Bloody marvellous", but honestly, what chance?'

'How do you know this, Jack?'

It was a question you were always very welcome to ask Lamb, and always you got no answer at all, or a token. He said: 'This was overheard, I believe.'

'By? Where, Jack? Someone talking aloud about an assassination effort, for God's sake. Where, Jack?'

'It must have been some isolated place.'

Harpur thought. 'Is that why you're suddenly off the army spots?'

'This could be the connection with Stan and mother and Helen,' Lamb replied.

'What?' Harpur muttered. 'What? That I don't follow.'

The children wanted Jack to give some more pursuit. 'I'm tired,' he said. 'My friend's keen. He's a professional.' Harpur joined the caper for three or four turns. The kids did not get so much out of this. Harpur was big but lacked Jack's terrifying bulk. To be chased by Harpur was to be chased by a man. Lamb was something from a child's nightmares or from folklore or both. Harpur rejoined Jack as one of his insignia'd camouflage shirts was pressed for a moment against the glass door, fringed with suds.

'This lad will get killed, won't he, Col?' Lamb replied. 'Look, I was offended when you went to him for insights, obviously. Very. And hurt. Badly. But this is a nobody kid who thinks he's great, and someone like Claud will eat him. I can't vamoose abroad and leave the boy wide open, his bird pregnant. Call it grasses' solidarity. He's looking for a bit of vengeance and a bit of self-protection. Plus there's business competition. They're all queuing for the Kenward inheritance, aren't they: Keith, Stanfield, Beau, Claud, Harry, Gerry? Possibly Panicking, I hear. Maybe others. Vine hasn't got the stature. He's doomed.'

The two children from the chase approached Lamb smiling their friendship and with fine synchronization one punched him hard in the left ear and one in the right. They ran back to their mother and Lamb waved a fist as they left. 'He's been into Claud's house already, stalking,' he said.

'How the hell can you know that? More overheard? Where?'

'This boy might be a very skilful burglar, but Claud's going to see signs. There's a volley waiting, or something slower.'

'Where was Claud when the lad visited?'

'On retreat?'

In a while they emptied their machines. 'You'd think my mother would understand about ageing and its degrading imperatives, wouldn't you, Col, being old? She can't see how lucky her defunct son is to have a girl like Helen, can't see that somehow I've got to keep her and keep her happy, do some compromising. You'd appreciate this, wouldn't you? How long do you reckon you'll hold on to Denise, a mind and body like hers and you in your state?'

Harpur went home via the street where Becky and Vine lived. Iles was watching on his own and had just arrived. 'They've gone out somewhere together, dressed up,' the ACC said. Harpur felt relieved. It might mean they were occupied for the rest of the night, and Keith would not try his hunting mission yet. Harpur believed that to get yourself a private life, you took some risks with clientèle.

Denise was still there when Harpur returned. The talk had gone back to *Casablanca*. Hazel said: 'That famous scene where the Germans sing their fatherland song and then the band plays the Marseillaise was in *La Grand Illusion* five years earlier.'

'And the *Casablanca* croupier's in both pictures,' Denise replied.

'Iles is always on about *Casablanca*,' Jill said. 'Why Hazel's been swotting up. How come you know so much about it, Denise?'

'She knows everything,' Harpur said.

'Not where you went tonight,' Jill replied. 'Or your next career move.'

The four of them played knockout whist for the rest of the evening. On her way to bed, Jill said: 'See you at breakfast, then, Denise.'

'You'll stay? Are they rushing you?' Harpur asked, once they were alone.

'I think I like it.'

'Well, I do,' he said.

'But I refuse to be a mother-figure.'

'They wouldn't let you, love.'

In bed, just before they slept, Denise said: 'Helen's

200

going to the States for a while with Jack. To get her away from Stan Stanfield.'

'Oh?'

'She was in two minds, but she's going.'

'Why?'

'Because she loves Jack, I suppose. Yes. Stan's just a gorgeous giggle. Very gorgeous, but a giggle.'

'He sounds grand.'

'You must know him. Shady. Big moustache.'

'That what tickles Helen?'

'You knew this already, did you, Colin?'

Chapter 28

Next night, Harpur and Iles watched Vine's place together. Iles seemed mild and edgeless, like someone sick. He even discussed signs of his wife Sarah's devotion to him, and the satisfaction they both drew from love of their child. Harpur sat on the yawns. 'To revere family values is not necessarily to be a cunt like Mark Lane, Col, is it?' Iles remarked.

'I know several other people who believe in the family, sir.' Harpur wondered if the ACC had applied for a Chief's post elsewhere and was rehearsing normality for the interview. At just before midnight Keith came out hurriedly and got into his car. He was wearing his combat jacket.

'For once I think I'll tail Vine,' Harpur said.

Alongside him in the front of the Ital, Iles immediately tensed and grew more recognizable. 'Why?' he asked. 'I thought the girl was your worry.'

'I worry about both, sir. Strictly, it's Keith we have the debt to.'

'Debt? Don't muck me about, Harpur. Little Keith has killed a postie. Maybe a guard.'

'I think I'll watch him,' Harpur replied. He started the old car, taken from the pool for anonymity. Iles's Ford was around the corner. 'I'll drop you at your vehicle, shall I, sir?'

'You've got information again, have you, you hoarding, slippery sod?' The ACC had begun to yell and Harpur rolled up the window once more. 'You know where he's going, yes? They're not coming here. *He's* going to *them*. Is he mad? See him do a finger check inside his jacket, inventorying the gun? It will be the Smith and Wesson 645, the moron. I'm coming with you.'

Christ. Harpur drove after Keith. Harpur had thought if real trouble started he could call aid. Iles would not want that. The detective was dead but the execution squad wasn't, and he intended to be it, or at least half. Uneasily, Harpur recalled the finger pistol. Maybe the ACC saw a chance at last to die valorously. 'This could be delicate, sir.'

'You're saying real close contact at last, Harpur?'

'There might be numbers.'

'I love it,' Iles replied. He had resumed the gentle, lilting voice used for his tender thoughts about Sarah and their little girl. 'What I've always loathed, Colin, is one-to-one shooting. That means malice, coldness, so against my grain.' He stared after Vine's car. 'This is the way to Claud's place, yes?'

'It could be. We might need help.'

'Oh? People shouting "Armed police"? That's always seemed to me bombastic and self-defeating, Harpur.'

Keith Vine parked in the next street to Claud's house. Harpur was expecting it and had already pulled in a long way back when Vine stopped.

Iles said: 'You've got this whole thing scheduled to a T, haven't you, you little clairvoyant, you?'

Keith paused in the car for about a minute, possibly checking again whatever he had aboard, and thinking how Becky would eternally adore him after this killing. Then they watched him walk from the vehicle and turn the corner. But it was not a walk. A throbbing strut. He knew he would win and grab a cheerful future for Becky and the child, even if nobody else knew it. Harpur and Iles followed. As Iles said, neither of them could hope to tail unseen, especially in empty night streets. Harpur was too burly for the role anyway, anywhere, any time. Although Keith seemed so thrilled with himself that he never looked back, they had to give him plenty of room, and it worried Harpur. Keith had no protection at this distance. All right, he did not deserve much from Harpur any longer, but could you let a kid, blinded by ego and due to be a dad, fall into a three-against-one, and one of the three Claud? By the time they turned the corner after Vine, he was out of sight.

They separated. Iles went to the other side of the street. They walked fast towards Claud's semi, keeping level with each other. It had been Harpur's idea, but he thought now they were probably more noticeable like this than if they had stayed together: Jehovah's Witnesses on some small-hours leafleting? When he reached the house, Harpur immediately turned into its bit of drive and made for the rear garden. He heard Iles not far behind. They had to be speedy. Whatever might happen to Keith could happen instantly. Of course, Iles would argue it might not happen to Keith, but to Claud, if Keith was as good as he thought, and that nobody ought to hinder this. But Harpur took Lamb's estimate. Jack thought Claud and friends would be waiting for Vine and that he had no chance. So did Harpur. Whether Lamb gave a fact or an opinion you'd better believe it. He would be missed.

Claud was not somebody to have ordinary locks on his house and Harpur assumed Vine would try a window. But he found nothing to show entry on any at the back. When he turned the handle of the kitchen door it opened. Keith had provided himself with a key somehow? This could not be a plastic card job. Or perhaps Claud had left it unlocked deliberately, a 'beckon', as these lads called it, when trapping. But surely to God Vine would know about beckons and realize he was expected. Of course, with his ripe belief in himself he might carry on anyway. In his shoulder holster he would have some weapon to convince himself he could take on the world. Babes were often like this when they bought their first gun, and on top, Keith had the triumph of his job on the postie's chest to keep his spirits bright. The weapon might be that S and W 645. Harpur doubted it.

The house was dark downstairs, but a light burned in one of the bedrooms or the bathroom. Harpur would have liked to know the house layout. It could easily have been found in the time since he spoke to Jack. Harpur wondered if he was slowing up. Hadn't Lamb asked how long he would be able to hold on to Denise? Stuff Lamb. Why hadn't *he* come up with the house details? Normally that would be standard. Jack must be getting end-of-term, dreaming of his US ramble with an unshared Helen, maybe.

Claud was between girls and living alone, Harpur knew that much. And tonight, now, Claud would like it believed that he had retired and was at his prayers before sleep, or reading something unputdownable by Aeschylus or Rushdie. Iles had caught up with Harpur and they stood together just into the kitchen. Even in the dark, Harpur could see Iles was worried by the open rear door. He had bent to examine the two first-class locks fitted there, neither damaged. Training taught you could meet no worse danger than on entering a dark house unasked, except when you climbed the stairs in that house and were on offer from below and above. Vine might have done both if he thought he could hit Claud in bed. Iles and Harpur might have to do both. The kitchen was designed in a very expensive, heavy mock-wood mode, and looked unkempt or filthy, used dishes everywhere, grease tugging fondly at Harpur's synthetic soles. It made a slight sucking sound at each step and could be a give-away.

A light came on suddenly downstairs and there was a shout and the sound of something metal hitting the floor, then a much heavier sound, almost certainly a body going down. A door to one of the rooms must be partly open and so was the kitchen door, letting in the triangle of light and the noise.

Claud spoke, out of sight but easily audible: 'Cuffs and cuts.' Harpur heard the click of handcuffs closing. 'We get Keithy into the shower and do some work on him when he comes round. See him off, but not fast. He can tell us this and that.'

'Like who's in it beside Stanfield and Beau,' Foster said.

'Like Harpur and Iles,' Gerry Reid said.

'All of it before he goes,' Claud replied. 'He'll be easy. There's a set of kitchen knives out there. Select one each, and one for me. We all do this on him, a confed. job. Put his Makarov in your pocket, Gerry.'

Harpur saw Iles bring out the Bulldog Magnum and Harpur took the Colt from his pocket. Iles moved quickly alongside the door. In a couple of seconds Foster and Reid pushed it wide and switched on the kitchen light. Reid was holding what could be a Mauser automatic pointed towards the ground. Foster had a piece of piping with a brass nut at one end. Harpur thought he made out blood and hair on the brass. At once, Iles struck down hard with the Bulldog on Reid's wrist and the automatic clattered to the ground. Then the ACC was gone from the kitchen in a couple of steps, out of view, and making towards the light. Harpur covered the two of them with the Colt. They had been too shocked to speak so far, but noise of the Mauser falling and Iles's dash must have carried and Claud shouted: 'What's happening out there?' Immediately afterwards he yelled, 'Christ!'

'Sort of,' Iles replied.

Harpur heard what might be a heavy blow followed once more by the sound of perhaps a body toppling to the floor. A couple of seconds later came the noise of one shot from the lighted room. Startled, Harpur turned his head and body and the Colt a fraction, as he tried to see after Iles. On the edge of his vision, he was aware of Foster raising the lump of piping and about to rush him.

He swung back to face the two of them, and pointed the Colt at Harry's chest: 'Put it on the draining board, Harry. And the Makarov, Gerry.' They hesitated and Harpur jabbed the Colt towards them in the air, something you were told never to do: a gun was a gun, not a boxing glove, and should be kept still and steady, preferably in two hands. Foster snarled but moved no nearer and in a moment placed the piece of piping among meat scraps on a dirty plate. Reid put the Makarov alongside. 'Now, both of you come past me slowly but not near, and go to the other end of the kitchen,' Harpur said. They did it. Harpur kept them covered and backed towards where the Mauser had fallen at Reid's feet. He picked it up. Things were taking much too long. He was anxious about Iles alone in the other room, and not alone. 'Now come back,' he told Reid and Foster. They moved past him again towards the door and, with a gun in each hand, he prodded them out of the kitchen ahead of him and fully shielding him, towards the lighted room.

Vine was unconscious on his stomach near the door, arms handcuffed behind his back, a circle of blood in his hair. On the floor not far from him Claud Beyonton lay face up, but unrecognizable, those mouse-features broken and badly jumbled. The wall behind him was heavily spattered. A big automatic lay on the carpet about fifteen feet from the body.

'How?' Reid cried.

Crouched down, Iles was searching Beyonton's pockets for the handcuff keys. 'Always the *mot* fucking *juste*, and usually more than one, Gerry,' he said over his shoulder. 'Claud has committed suicide by a shot in the mouth.' He pointed at the automatic. 'Looks to me very like the Smith and Wesson 645 we have in mind, Harpur. He must have known the law was closing in on him for those two deaths. Yes. Although Claud might appear piffling he was essentially big, and did the big thing at his end, as one would expect. So significant he used the mouth. Wasn't

207

the survivor guard quoted as saying a raider meant to kill him like that? This was an act of penance. He had depth, sensitivity. Echoes all round here: Gerry just now disarmed by a wrist-blow like one of the van raiders, I believe.'

Gravely and respectfully Iles straightened up and gave Claud a couple of ferocious kicks in the kidneys. 'He died alone,' the ACC said. 'Absolutely alone. When he's examined, I wouldn't mind betting there'll be signs of a savage beating to the body. Possibly there's been a clubbing blow to the head as well, though it's difficult to sort out the bruising now. My feeling is he told his present, new confeds, whoever they might be, yes, whoever – I fear we shall never know – told them that his fears meant he could not go on, wanted out, sick and ashamed of it all. Of course, those bastards would see this as betrayal and react in foul, violent style, poor hero. Right wrist damaged. That could be in the beating or that smack during the raid. Must have used the left to pop himself. He was so determined to end everything. Creditable marksmanship, wouldn't you say?

'Then, after this brutal treatment from them – possibly they thought him dead – oh, yes, I should think so – despite this, Claud somehow crawls home and seeks oblivion and a kind of belated, messy, yet, I think, valid honour.' He kicked Claud three or four times more in the side and gut with his Doc Martens. 'I expect he'll be found soon. I don't think we want to detain these two gems, do we, Col? They can't help us on this. You're lucky, boys. Think of Claud as having sacrificed himself in your place. See him in high, religious terms.'

Reid snarled: 'How come the gun's not in his hand, if he shot himself?'

Iles looked reproachful: 'Gerry, Gerry – recoil. A big-calibre pistol hardly ever stops in the hand of a suicide. One reason they were suspicious about the supposed self-slaughter of that Clinton aide. You must know that.'

'Well, *you'd* know it. Claud would never kill himself.'

'People said the same of Maxwell,' Iles replied. 'But if you like we could discuss the whole thing at the nick.'

Foster gave Reid a heavy nudge.

'Well, possibly he might,' Gerry said.

'It's bound to upset you,' the ACC replied, 'this is the loss of a British gentleman.'

Vine began to come round.

Iles bent over him and undid the cuffs: 'Don't you realize, Keithy, you could even now be sleeping spoons, nursing one of the sweetest arses I've seen since bonfire night? No, maybe not quite that long. Since – it would be around December 2. But we do like you. You serve a purpose.'

Chapter 29

'Well, here's a real turn-up, sir,' Iles cried. 'They find a shady lad called Leonard Claud Beyonton, whom of course we know, dead from what appears to be a self-inflicted gunshot wound, and first tests suggest it's the very weapon that did the sub-postmaster and a security guard on the bank van raid across the frontier. That crew over there wouldn't give us their toe jam, but I don't see why we can't act large and tell them what we know. Well, rather as Claud himself acted large, ultimately. Not *The Mouse That Roared* but the mouse that fell on its sword.'

'Is this conclusive, Desmond?' Lane asked. He looked from the ACC to Harpur, then back to the ACC, in that tortured, pitiable way he had once Iles really got going. The three of them were in Harpur's room, the Chief wearing one of his least pretentious suits and again shoeless.

Iles said: 'Not conclusive yet, sir. Tests. *Virtually* conclusive.'

'Did Beyonton seem a suicidal type?' Lane asked.

'Some of these people are more feeling than might seem, sir,' Iles replied.

'Do they move from something so small-scale as the post office raid to an attack on an armoured van?' the Chief asked.

'It probably seemed quite large-scale to the postie, sir,' Iles replied. 'Lads like Claud, if they're short of readies, do what's nearest and easiest. Isn't that so, Col?'

'They sometimes knock off a small job for gun money,' Harpur replied.

'Gun money?' Lane asked.

The Chief had once been a great detective but liked to talk now as though he had left behind and forgotten the rough detail of villain procedures, as if to ignore it was to wipe it out. Iles would do an imitation of him with an imagined telescope to his blind eye and saying, 'I see no shit.'

Iles played along: 'They pick a small-take target so they can afford to buy or hire for something juicier,' Iles said. 'We're still looking for Leyton Harbinger, the usual armourer from The Hobart, aren't we Col?'

'Is that the big pub on a corner, with the parrot?' Harpur replied.

'They want four for the van raid, don't they?' Lane asked. 'Was Beyonton still operating with Reid and Foster?'

Iles smiled a congratulation. 'Your memory and sharpness, sir, if I may say! We would very much like them for it, obviously. But both are well alibied, I'm afraid. Claud would seem to have new companions. We've done as much as we can on that. It's not our case.'

'And the fourth?' Lane asked.

'I love the thoroughness, the relentlessness with which you would wish to pursue offenders, sir. I hope our neighbouring colleagues have it, though I fear not.'

'And still I hear nothing from our – from our helper, Vine, or his partner,' Lane said.

'Col thinks there could be development there. Yes, Harpur?'

'One way or the other,' he replied.

Chapter 30

At home in bed with Denise again at the weekend, Harpur thought he heard a noise downstairs. He did not wake her, but went out on to the landing and listened. From there he could recognize the sound, a coin beating an occasional pattern against glass. He went down and let Keith Vine in by the door to the garden.

'Same bird as last time?' Keith asked. 'I saw you and her go in, but too far off to recognize. Or a change? Sleep naked? I don't blame you.'

Harpur brought a raincoat for himself from the hall.

'I won't keep you,' Keith said.

They sat down in the living room and Harpur made up a couple of gin and ciders. 'You've decided to leave after all, have you?' Harpur asked. 'You and Becky. That's fine. The offer's still there. The Chief mentioned it only the other day.'

'Look, the way all that was arranged the other night,' Vine replied. 'I don't understand it, not a bit, but I'm so grateful.' He put a hand up and touched his scalp.

'Is it still France?' Harpur asked.

'Their partnership is finished. Well, clearly,' Vine said. 'Claud gone. The other two are nothing.'

'I think you're wise to get out,' Harpur replied.

The living-room door opened slowly and Jill, wearing pyjamas, came in. 'Hazel and I heard something,' she said.

'Us,' Harpur replied. 'Just a chat.'

'Hazel thought Iles,' she said, looking about very sleep-

212

ily. 'She sent me to see. She's scared of seeming obvious. You know Hazel and her corny pride.'

'No, not Mr Iles. My friend here is a book dealer. He might want to take the whole lot.' Harpur waved his hand towards the shelves. 'That would please you, wouldn't it?'

Jill yawned enormously and said: 'I want to keep the Joe Orton *Diaries* and that one on boxing, *The Sweet Science*. All that Mrs Gaskell stuff and both Eliots, out. Why have you got your coat on in the house?'

'You can go back to sleep now, love, can't you?' Harpur answered.

Jill shivered and then, after a moment, seemed to wake up a bit. She gazed at Keith. 'This is Becky's boyfriend, yes? Nothing to do with the books? But he doesn't seem fink. His face too square, and the chin.'

Keith looked appalled and obviously thought he had better do something fast for his identity. He went to gaze fondly at the library. 'What I love about books is you get all sorts of titles,' he said. 'I've noticed that before.'

'Yes, the fink,' Jill replied. 'So, why don't you take care of Becky properly, and the baby?'

Vine, still at the shelves, turned quickly to stare at her. He was angry. 'Listen, little girl, I—'

Jill said: 'I should think Dad will have to do you for something before long. That's how you look to me. And how Dad is.'

'Goodnight, Jill,' Harpur said.

She left. 'What's that mean, Mr Harpur?' Keith asked. ' "Do me for something before long". My God, you talk to your kids about me?'

'So why are you here, then, Keith?' Harpur replied.

Keith pointed the chin and came to sit down again. 'It's a bit, well, sensitive.'

'You want more than we've offered?' Harpur sighed and nodded. 'I shouldn't tell you, but the sum is elastic, as long as you can prove the extra's vital. The Chief's very humane.'

Vine's voice went shaky and hurried: 'I don't know if I want to talk about it – after what your kid just said.' His breathing had become noisy. 'How can you do me? Claud carries the can for everything, doesn't he? His 645. Hazel's the one I already met? Young, even for Iles?'

Harpur waited.

Eventually, Vine said: 'A tale around for quite a time now that you and Mr Iles were, well, in a very unofficial way, obviously, connected, or sort of in touch with, Claud's business. Look, don't get me wrong, I know it's only a tale, and very, well, unofficial. Obviously. That Mrs McCallion.'

'You're not leaving the patch?' Harpur replied.

Vine handled his scalp again. 'Why I said I didn't understand what went on at Claud's place the other night. If you and Iles were confed. with Claud, how was it—? Oh, I know Mr Iles says suicide and nobody will say different. But— Myself, I'm unconscious while all that happened. But— Well, Mr Harpur, I mean.'

'You're not going to France?' Harpur replied.

Keith stood and began to pace slowly like the chairman of the board, his glass in his hand. 'What I wondered, and with the hearty agreement of certain associates, was, in view of the collapse of Claud's firm, and of possible antagonisms within that firm, as witness Claud's undisputably violent death – I wondered if you and Mr Iles would consider taking an interest in another little team. Little yet extremely sound. Believe me, this is a very solid outfit, with the capital already up front. I mean, I've seen it, touched it. I'd give an affidavit to that, if things in this business were ever written down. All right, so Claud's company put some funds together by a special effort. But what I'm saying is, this other outfit, well, the funds were available right off, from the start, real reserves. This is stability. This is cred.

'Another tale is Claud's syndicate let some fourth member hold all the capital meant for future dealing and he's still holding it, won't let it go now Claud's dead. As a matter of fact, I could put a name to him, but would I grass? Just let's say someone lucky. Even if those two wanted to go on and were capable, they can't.' Putting the proposition had settled him and his breathing was back to normal now. 'Full confidentiality would be maintained, naturally. Rest assured. Please, please, don't see this as an attempt to bind you in, so you couldn't act against us, Mr Harpur. Well, I think you know Keith Vine better than that. This is a business matter, that's all.'

Keith sat down again and Harpur leaned across and pulled open the zip on his combat jacket. 'Makarov? That's got to be Leyton. Where the hell is he, Keith?'

'Leyton?'

'From The Hobart.'

'That the big pub on a corner, with the parrot?' Keith replied.

'Old Amy there fancied you a bit, I expect. Might she have pushed that used 645 to Claud, to ease any trouble away from you?'

The door opened and Denise appeared wearing one of Harpur's shirts as a nightdress. 'I woke up and you were gone, Col,' she said.

'It's all right. My friend's leaving now,' Harpur said.

Vine said: 'But, now wait, Mr Harpur. This deal. I mean, about the books.'

'He's leaving now,' Harpur replied, getting out of his chair.

'I'll go by the back way,' Keith said. 'Just can't wait for each other? Nice. Well, you're entitled.'

After he had gone, Denise said: 'One of your grasses?'

'You're really settling into this household.'